HELL'S
Wedding Bells

ANNABELLE
ANDERS

IN FOR
A PENNY

Hell's Wedding Bells

Cover Art by Forever After Romance Designs

Photography: Period Images/ Shutterstock

❀ Formatted with Vellum

A NOTE TO THE READER

Hells Wedding Bells was originally published in the 2019 anthology, *Once Upon a Christmas Wedding*.

As always, to my readers. Because my stories become real only when I can share them. Happy Reading!
Love,
Annabelle

TILL DEATH

*I*f only she'd been born a man.

Lady Lila Breton, the eldest daughter of the Earl of Quimbly, would have rather been almost anyone else on that sunny but cold December morning.

Or *anywhere* else, for that matter. She scrunched her nose in frustration.

She'd long ago given up on running away from her father's home, from his outbursts, his unreasonable expectations, and his outrageous demands. Although the idea presented itself from time to time, she just as quickly dismissed it, having no money, no skills, and nowhere to go.

And besides, running away would require that she abandon her mother and her younger sister, Arianna.

She could not leave them alone to cope with Father's madness.

"You should wear something pretty today, my lady." Fran, her ladies' maid for the past ten years, held up a silk rose-colored gown for Lila's inspection. "It's your wedding, after all. You ought to look pretty for your groom."

"A groom I've never met and who cares nothing about me as a person, how much do you think my father is paying him?" This was her second betrothal, the first one having lasted for most of her life, only to come to an abrupt end when her betrothed ended up marrying another woman. From what she understood, the lady had been a homely bluestocking. Miss Emily Goodnight had married the Earl of Blakely, thwarting the betrothal that had been in place for as long as Lila could remember.

When the betrothal had ended, her father had moved them away from the home they'd always known, away from the few friends she'd managed to make, and up to a distant estate near the Irish Sea that she'd barely known existed. Nearly as far north as one could go and not end up in Scotland. In fact, Gretna Green was not far off.

Her father had forbidden them from making the short journey into the nearby village of Burnbridge even once, keeping her and her sister from having any sort of social life whatsoever. They could not take part in any church gatherings, town assemblies, or ladies' socials.

Nothing.

It was difficult not to think of herself as a prisoner.

Lila stared in the mirror, feeling none of the emotions a bride ought to be feeling. Her only excitement came from the fact that she would soon be free of her father.

Which presented her with a new set of worries.

She exhaled loudly.

Her prospective groom was the Duke of Pemberth. She would be a duchess, no less. She'd never heard of the dukedom until the night before when her father had informed her of their appointment today.

Not an appointment for the man to pay his addresses.

An appointment with a clergyman and two witnesses.

She'd been given no choice in the matter.

"Not the rose," Lila answered, feeling frustrated and powerless. "The brown muslin."

"Oh, my lady, not that one. I've mended it more times than I can count. It's the most atrocious gown you own."

"Precisely."

Lila reached up and began pulling her hair into a tight and unimaginative chignon. It would emphasize the dark circles beneath her eyes. And yes, if she pinched her lips just so, she could appear even older than her six and twenty years.

Any man who transacted business with her father could not be much better himself. Honor was for the weak in her father's mind. Money and status were all that mattered.

And beauty.

Fran made some disapproving noises but returned the rose gown to Lila's wardrobe and then withdrew the brown one from an old trunk.

"Leave the wrinkles," Lila ordered. "And I'll wear the green shawl Mama made for me last Christmas."

Utterly appropriate, with the holidays less than a month away. Her mother had used two colors of green: moss and bright parakeet.

Lila lifted her arms as Fran assisted her into the dress and studied herself in the looking glass. She smiled tightly. Oh, yes. This ensemble was most appropriate. She had no idea why a duke would deign to marry her. There must be a great deal of money involved. She'd do nothing to sweeten his bargain.

A knock sounded on the door, and her mother entered without waiting for permission.

"Oh, Lila." She met Lila's eyes in the reflection of the mirror. "He's not going to be happy with you at all."

He.

Her father.

Lila grimaced. She resembled her mother a great deal. Slim and with the same blue eyes, both stood barely over five feet tall, and, until the last few years, had shared the same color of hair. Glossy mahogany, as her mother liked to call it.

"He'll have no reason to care one way or the other, presumably, after this morning." *If the duke does not cry off upon seeing me.* And what if he went ahead with the marriage? A shiver of apprehension slid down Lila's spine. What if he was old? What if he was very young? She'd imagined all sorts of horrifying scenarios while trying to sleep the night before.

His estate was located even farther north, yet remained in England. But instead of facing the Irish Sea, it was located on the opposite coast.

She wondered if the North Sea would bring her the same solace she found along the shores of Bryony Manor. Perhaps they all looked the same... water and sky.

If the duke did not call off, Lila would have to leave her mother and sister. But she would do everything within her power to convince her new husband to send for them. If not her mother, at least Arianna.

"Will Arianna be allowed to be present... for the ceremony?" Lila would feel only slightly better if her sister could be there.

But her mother was already shaking her head. "She's not to miss her lessons."

Lila had guessed as much.

"Fran. I'd like a moment alone with my daughter."

Lila hadn't expected her mother to attempt any sort of mother-daughter pre-wedding heart to heart. She met her maid's gaze in the mirror and shrugged.

Fran finished fastening her gown from the back and then dropped the ghastly shawl around her shoulders. Her mother frowned in further disappointment but did not object as the maid took her leave.

"You don't need to—" Lila would save her mother such embarrassment, but her mother raised one hand and then gestured for her to sit down in the high-backed velvet chair at the end of the bed.

Lila lowered herself in place, and her mother stood facing her, hands hidden in her deep skirt pockets.

"I know little of this Pemberth, whom your father has called here to marry you. But I've seen him." Clamping her lips together tightly, she stared out the window for a moment, as though she'd forgotten she was even speaking.

"Mother?" Lila reached up and touched her mother's hand.

Her mother blinked and then nodded slowly. "I want you to take this. Hide it with your jewels, and if you ever have need of subduing your husband, simply sprinkle this into his food."

She withdrew one hand from her pocket and held out a velvet drawstring bag for Lila to take.

"What is it?" Lila took it, wondering if this was how her own mother had managed to survive her father all these years.

Her mother's eyes seemed unfocused and then she blinked again. "A sleeping potion. Only use it if you fear him. Do you understand?"

She'd never seen her own father actually act out in violence toward another soul, her mother included, but she'd heard rumors that he'd committed atrocities. She did her best to imagine the rumor held little, if any, truth.

Her imagination never grew powerful enough to believe it.

Yes, she could understand her mother's concern. Nodding, she took the little cloth bag from her mother and then stuffed it into the back of her valise.

She prayed she'd never need it.

Strangely, her mother took Lila by the shoulders and leaned forward, dropping a kiss on each cheek. "I love you, Lila. I want you to know that I've done my best for you and Arianna. Please, always remember that."

Lila nodded. "Of course. It cannot have been easy for you." And then she added, "I love you too, Mama." But this wasn't going to be goodbye forever. She'd make certain of it, no matter what she had to do to procure her husband's cooperation.

"Best not to dawdle." Her mother brushed at Lila's sleeves and then tucked a stray hair behind her ear. "They await you downstairs."

Feeling as though her limbs had suddenly gone numb, Lila nodded again.

She had no idea what she was walking into. *If you are there, God, please let him be a decent man. He doesn't need to be smart, or an appropriate age, or handsome even.* She cared not one fig if he was charming and affable. All she could hope for was that he would be kind.

What was the chance of that?

Fear sent ice coursing through her veins as she followed

her mother downstairs. Perhaps it would be best if he took one look at her and changed his mind.

Because as horrible as her present circumstances were, better the devil you know than the one that you don't.

She caught sight of herself in a large mirror in the foyer.

The gown was delightfully wrinkled. And the bright green yarn of the shawl made her skin appear almost yellow.

Stunning.

VINCENT SAINT-PIERRE, the Duke of Pemberth, would rather be anywhere but Lord Quimbly's library that morning.

Since his older brother Keenan's untimely death three months ago, Vincent's life had been irrevocably altered. *Death*. His heart curdled inside at the word. *Suicide*. He would not ignore the truth.

After driving the dukedom deeply into debt and then gambling away anything left of value, Keenan had not even had the decency to remain on this earth to face the consequences of his actions.

No, he'd left that for Vincent.

A penniless dukedom, a broken-down estate, and now this.

The promise to marry Quimbly's daughter sight unseen.

His brother's vowels had not died with him. No, they, too, had been bequeathed to Vincent.

He'd like to hate his brother for it, if only he hadn't loved the benighted fool.

A noise at the door had him turning in some curiosity.

The older woman, he presumed to be the countess. She was followed by a timid-looking creature wearing a color that offended his eyes. Good God.

Beneath the hideous garments appeared to be a shapeless form, part of the hem dragging behind her as she shuffled into the room, head ducked meekly.

He barely contained a groan.

But of course, his brother had saddled him with an antidote. Not that it mattered, he supposed. He'd likely be too busy working his own land to seek any satisfaction with her.

Although he'd require an heir.

Vincent made no comment, choosing instead to bow toward the countess.

Lord Quimbly wasn't so considerate. "Good God, Lila. It isn't going to work. Step over here, this instant."

It was her—his betrothed—Lady Lila. The name hinted at a feminine beauty he'd not seen so far.

She hesitated only an instant before doing as the earl bid.

Before she made it halfway across the room, however, her father had stepped forward to tug at the shawl before then tearing it off of her shoulders. She nearly lost her balance at the violence of his gesture.

"Now, here." Vincent stepped forward. "That's not necessary."

"I know my daughter, Pemberth. She's doing this on purpose." And with his other hand, his fingers delved into the back of her head. The girl covered her face with her hands while Quimbly, *her father*, dragged out a few pins, releasing the twisted mane to tumble down her back to just past her waist.

With one last motion, the earl forced the girl to drop her hands. "See. Not so bad." Quimbly tilted her chin up and turned her face in Vincent's direction with some satisfaction.

Vincent swallowed hard.

Her beauty stunned him. His soon-to-be wife.

Cobalt blue eyes glared at him.

The clergyman Lord Quimbly had summoned rose from where he'd planted himself earlier. "Are we ready to begin, then?"

Keenan had promised to make Quimbly's daughter a duchess as an ante in a game of cards. And then he had lost. If Vincent didn't make good on his brother's promise, the Pemberth title would not only be penniless but without honor as well.

Vincent nodded.

A small cry came from the girl, who'd dropped her gaze once again.

"My lady." The collared man gestured to the defiant young woman. "You stand here, beside His Grace. And Lord and Lady Quimbly shall act as witnesses."

The girl's mother nudged her forward until she was standing beside Vincent, her reluctance so strong he would swear he could feel it burning along his side.

Vincent dropped his gaze as well, ashamed to be a part of such a sordid affair. *Damn you, Keenan.*

He barely made out the words on the book the vicar clutched before the man opened it and began performing the ceremony. *The Book of Common Prayer.*

Not much godliness going into this marriage.

"Dearly beloved, we are gathered together here in the sight of God…"

Vincent glanced sideways in time to see Lady Lila raise a handkerchief to her mouth.

She clenched her hands so tightly, her knuckles appeared white, and he was almost certain that she was crying. Should he put a halt to the proceedings? All of this was quite beyond his realm. He'd be far better at comforting his livestock than an unwilling bride.

"I require and charge you both, as ye will answer at the dreadful day of judgment when the secrets of all hearts shall be disclosed...." The clergyman's tone was even and steady. "For be ye well assured, that so many as are coupled together otherwise than God's Word doth allow are not joined together by God; neither is their matrimony lawful."

Would her mother stop the ceremony? If Lady Lila was so disinclined to marry him, why did she not speak up herself?

Quimbly was the only person in the room who appeared satisfied with the proceedings.

"Your Grace, Vincent Sebastian Lucifer Saint-Pierre, wilt thou have this woman to thy wedded wife, to live together after God's ordinance in the holy estate of matrimony? Wilt thou love her, comfort her, honor, and keep her in sickness and in health; and, forsaking all others, keep thee only unto her, so long as ye both shall live?"

Vincent swallowed around a huge lump that had appeared in his throat. "I will." He'd never taken a vow he did not feel confident he could keep.

He glanced down at the woman standing beside him.

Until that moment.

"And my lady, Lila Catherine Breton, wilt thou have this man to thy wedded husband, to live together after God's ordinance in the holy estate of matrimony? Wilt thou obey him, and serve him, love, honor, and keep him in sickness and in health; and, forsaking all others, keep thee only unto him, so long as ye both shall live?"

The room fell uncomfortably silent until his bride jumped. Vincent suspected a sharp elbow had landed on her ribcage at the same time her mother shot her a stern warning look. Lady Lila responded in a thin voice, "I will."

Quimbly mumbled something in satisfaction. When asked about rings, it was her father who handed them over.

His bride's icy cold hand trembled as she slid the cool metal circle upon Vincent's finger. He noticed how small and delicate her hand was compared to his.

The remainder of the ceremony passed in a blur.

The next thing he knew, he'd signed his name on a license and Quimbly was showing the clergyman the door.

Vincent had planned on staying the night at Bryony Manor initially but having already spent more time than he'd prefer in Quimbly's company, he decided he'd rather take to the road and stop at an inn along the way.

Along with his less than enthusiastic bride.

A servant chose that moment to enter. "The nuncheon is served, my lord."

"Oh, yes. Indeed. You must be hungry, Your Grace? From your travels?" Lady Quimbly lacked the maniacal force of her husband and seemed to wish to bring some normalcy to the situation. She was petite like her daughter but rather than hold her shoulders proudly, she hunched over.

Vincent did not have the heart to refuse her. "I would be grateful for the meal but we've several miles to cover and cannot take long." He turned to address his... wife. "I hope you have already packed. I'd like to get on the road shortly after, however, as I'm needed at Glenn Abby."

"But—" she started to interrupt, showing more life than she had since she'd first presented herself.

"I've already been away longer than I ought," Vincent added. Which was mostly true. His steward would require his assistance in the fields, what with three of his tenants having up and left for the Americas after Keenan's death. Not to mention the accounting books he'd put off, a task he barely tolerated.

Vincent was not much of a numbers man.

Hell, truth be told, he wasn't much of a books man either.

He was far more comfortable in the pastures, atop his horse.

The earl scowled at his daughter. "Lady Lila's maid can have her belongings prepared immediately." And then, waving at Vincent, he said, "This way, Your Grace."

"*Her* Grace," Vincent corrected the earl. "She is no longer *Lady Lila*."

The earl turned back, eyes narrowed.

Vincent had not appreciated the manner in which Quimbly had treated his daughter, and as his wife now, she was entitled to Vincent's protection. The earl would treat her with all due respect.

Vincent knew nothing of who she was; her thoughts, her likes and dislikes, nor her dreams. But she'd taken vows to live the rest of her life as his duchess and he would make certain she was afforded the deference that came as a result.

By God, he didn't have much, but he had his honor.

And so would she.

HUSBAND

*H*e was huge. Not just tall and certainly not fat. He was just… huge. Thick blond hair curled atop his head, hanging practically into his eyes and onto his neck. He looked as though he hadn't been shaved in a week.

He looked like no duke Lila had ever known.

And yet, there was no mistaking his noble birth. It clung to him, despite his worn clothing and rough exterior. Something in the cool blue of his eyes and his chiseled features.

The top of her head did not even reach his shoulders, and she would guess he weighed over fifteen stones.

Dear God, this giant of a man was her husband. The thought both chilled and heated her blood at the same time.

"Fran will be coming as well." This was not a question on her part. "My maid. I cannot be without my maid." She lifted her chin and met his eyes for the first time as his wife. Lila would not be blindly submissive, as her mother had been. And it was important she begin as she intended to go forth. Gritting her teeth, she prepared herself to fight him on this point.

"But of course," he agreed without batting an eyelash, taking the wind out of her sails in an instant. "In fact, she can ride in the luggage coach as soon as she's packed all of your belongings. It won't be necessary for her to rush."

How dare he be so agreeable?

Nuncheon passed much as any other meal Lila had ever taken with her father. He did most of the talking, boasting to the duke of other noble acquaintances as well as travels he'd undertaken in his youth. Lila would have liked to learn something about her husband—her thoughts faltered at the word—but the man was not much of a talker.

He nodded and gave mostly monosyllabic answers. By the time they'd finished eating, she knew little more of him than she had when she had presented herself for their wedding.

Except that he was a hearty eater and didn't seem much impressed by anything her father had to say.

Which, she grudgingly admitted to herself, boded well for him.

She took no part in the conversation, nor did her mother.

At the conclusion of the meal, he placed his napkin on the plate in front of him and rose. "Your Grace." It took a moment for Lila to realize he addressed her. "I'll have my coach brought around for you. Clouds in the west."

Lila glanced down at her gown. "Do you mind if I change... into more appropriate traveling clothes?" She'd fooled no one with her defiant choice of garment that morning. For the journey to her new home, she'd prefer to wear something less... weathered. She also needed to find Arianna. She could not leave without saying goodbye, without promising to send for her at her first opportunity.

She'd need to reassure her sister that everything was going to be fine.

"Be quick about it," he responded.

And as much as she'd have liked to challenge him on the command, she was intimidated by his gruff manner and massive size. All the while, in the back of her mind was the knowledge that she would lie with him, perhaps as soon as tonight.

She nodded and made haste as she ascended the stairway to where the nursery had been reconfigured into a classroom.

Would he expect her to perform her wifely obligations in a hastily made up chamber at some inn along the road?

She could claim to be having her monthlies.

He was a giant of a man. If he so chose, she'd have no hope of stopping him.

But that was not part of her plan.

Her heart raced as she arrived at the landing, and she could not attribute it wholly to her exertions.

She knew something of what a man and a woman did to make a baby. She wasn't a girl, after all. And yet... far too many gaps existed in her education.

She would not think of it now. Perhaps she could befriend him first. Now that she was stuck with him, she had no wish to give him cause to dislike her.

He was just... such a very *large* man!

Lila opened the door to where she knew she'd find her sister, and at the interruption, Arianna's governess, Mrs. Betts, glanced up and closed her book.

Arianna sprang out of her desk, looking more like she was barely twelve than her actual age of six and ten. "Did he go ahead with it?"

Biting her lip, Lila nodded. She needed to change her gown, and she hadn't much time to spare. "I'm leaving now. I've come to say goodbye but as soon as I am settled, I'm going to write to you."

"You're leaving already?" Arianna's eyes filled up with tears. "But that isn't fair at all! Please, Lila, take me with you!"

Lila grasped Arianna by the shoulders, insisting that her younger sister meet her gaze solemnly. "I do not know him, Ari. I need to make sure he's... a better man than father." She didn't want to scare her, but it would be no good to bring her sister away from their father if her husband was no better.

Or worse.

She didn't want Arianna to worry about her. She'd have enough to cope with here. "But I promise, as soon as I know, I will send for you." The two sisters had always been there for one another. This could not be goodbye. She'd find a way to be with her sister again.

She'd make certain of it.

Tears fell from Arianna's eyes, but she nodded. Unfortunately, they both comprehended, all too well, the weaknesses of men.

"If you have need of me, contact Fran's sister. Fran will write to her so that she knows my location." Lila took a piece of paper from Arianna's desk and proceeded to write down the instruction. She could not trust her father to facilitate any sort of communications between them in the future.

With one last glance at her sister's scowl, she added, "I need to go now. Stay out of trouble. Keep writing your stories, and we'll see one another soon."

In her sister's eyes, she saw the same fear Lila felt deep inside.

With a father like Quimbly, nothing was ever certain.

Lila could only hope her husband was not the same.

WHEN LILA WAS FINALLY READY, she'd already taken at least ten minutes longer than he'd allotted, perhaps closer to twenty, she burst out the front door. Her husband glanced down at her from atop a giant mare and then tucked a pocket watch back into his jacket. He looked fit to be tied.

"I'm sorry!" she gushed as she made her way carefully down to the carriage. Warmth suffused her neck and cheeks, and she knew her eyes must be red. "I had to say goodbye to my sister." She'd also had Fran pin her hair up again and wore one of her favorite straw bonnets and an indigo-colored wool coat. She'd donned a traveling gown made of a pale blue muslin while Fran packed her a small valise. With one last glance around her chamber, she'd scooped up a book she had been reading and tucked it under her arm.

But he was on a horse. "You are riding outside?"

Her husband gestured toward the coach, horses and driver waiting patiently. "You'll have your privacy."

So she would not be given an opportunity to know him better before nightfall.

"But I—" She bit her lip. "I'd hoped we could familiarize ourselves…" Her eyes dropped.

His eyes narrowed and his jaw ticked, as though he was grinding his teeth. "We'll stop before dark."

Sitting atop the horse, he had her imagining him as some

sort of Nordic God, but then just as quickly dismissed such a foolish notion.

"But I—"

"I expect you'll come to know me well enough." And then he jerked his chin, indicating for her to climb into the carriage while he turned to ride ahead.

Not the beginning she had in mind. Although after her appearance earlier that day, what did she expect? He likely already regretted taking on such an unfashionable wife.

One more glance behind him and then he urged his horse into a run.

Married less than three hours and already he was running away from her.

Married...

As the driver steered them off of her father's property, Lila might as well have been driving into another world. She was a wife now. She opened her book but for all the jostling could hardly focus on the pages.

The carriage hit one bump, and then another, and she nearly lurched off the bench onto the floor.

This ride already promised to be an unpleasant one.

WILL YOU?

*H*is new wife had a ladies' maid, of course. What other luxuries would she expect upon reaching Glenn Abby? Vincent imagined how she might view his home when they finally arrived. A cold, forbidding castle, built in the late fifteenth century, it didn't exactly present the most welcoming of sights. Keenan, nor Vincent's father, nor his grandfather before him had done much of anything in the way of repairs.

The foundation listed, birds dwelt in some of the corridors, and bitter drafts managed to find their way into every room throughout the wintertime, regardless of how much coal one shoveled into the hearths.

Would she expect well-dressed servants lined up to greet her? Formal dining every evening? A ball, hosted in her honor?

Vincent laughed to himself at that thought.

Lila Catherine was her name. And now she was a Saint-Pierre. Would the title of duchess feel as foreign to her as duke felt to him?

Likely, she'd been born and raised for such an undertaking.

He shook his head.

Damn Keenan. The woman was going to be miserable. His gut clenched at the thought that his brother ought to have been the one to marry her.

But Keenan had forfeited the dubious privilege.

"Hiya!" He urged his mount forward. Tonight, he'd make her his wife in truth.

Hopefully, he could afford a decent chamber at the inn he had in mind.

RELIEF FLOWED over Lila when the rolling sounds of the carriage slowed, indicating they were pulling into a coaching inn. She hoped so, anyhow. She rather felt as though every bone in her body had been jostled loose. If this hideously uncomfortable carriage had any springs at all, they'd obviously hardened and lost all flexibility long ago. Furthermore, the bench cushion, if one could call it that, was worn thinner than her coat.

She squashed down the miserable feelings surging up inside of her.

Lila was not one to complain. Long ago, she'd discovered it a useless endeavor. It didn't really matter, anyhow. A husband and wedding night loomed all too close.

She rolled her shoulders and rubbed the muscles in her neck and then glanced out the window. A two-story inn, built out of brick and mortar, stood visible in the glow of evening twilight.

He ought to be happy, at least. She grimaced to herself.

They'd arrived before nightfall. She sniffed and clutched tightly to the leather strap hanging on the sidewall.

Her physical discomfort was not the only reason for her distress. Unable to read, she'd had nothing to do but imagine innumerable scenarios of what her marriage was going to be like, and the cumulated effect of these scenarios had set her nerves decidedly on edge.

Although she'd not allowed herself to cry this morning, or at the ceremony, or even when she'd said goodbye to Arianna, the urge was becoming nearly too much to overcome.

The coach jarred to a halt and if she hadn't been holding tightly to the strap, she likely would have fallen onto the floor.

Would they share a chamber?

She closed her eyes and prayed for strength.

Sounds of horses and hostlers and all manner of gentlemen swarming about the yard reminded her that she'd gone months without seeing any crowds of people, or anyone at all other than her own family and her father's servants.

It ought to be exciting. Interesting even, but after the events of her day, all she wanted to do was crawl beneath a heavy counterpane and sleep.

She peered out the window to watch as another coach arrived and waited for one of the footmen to open the door and lower the step for her.

And waited some more.

With a frustrated sigh, she edged herself forward and resigned to open the door for herself. "Dratted good for nothing—!" She didn't ordinarily grumble, or curse for that matter, but she'd had quite enough of this day.

Rearranging her skirts, she crouched on her haunches, grasped the handle, leaned forward and—

Tumbled into a solid mass of man as the door flew out of her hand.

"Oomph." Her head crashed into him first, and then the rest of her body followed. As tall and firm and muscular as he was, he easily prevented her from experiencing a most embarrassing and painful landing on the cold, hard ground.

It was the perfect ending to an absolutely miserable journey. She would not cry.

All she could think to do was bury her face where he could not see her.

Which happened to be his chest.

"I didn't think anyone was coming to assist me." She spoke into his shirt and coat, which most likely rendered her explanation utterly incoherent.

Talkative man that he was, he merely grunted and lowered her feet to the ground. Her unsteady knees nearly gave out on her, most likely due to the jarring she'd endured throughout the day.

She did not release him immediately. He really was quite sturdy.

As anyone with his size ought to be.

A large hulking brawny stranger. She removed her hand quickly. He would put himself inside of her. Possibly very soon.

It ought to be the other way around, she fumed inside. Women oughtn't to have to suffer for the mere sake of... every damn thing that men wanted.

Again, she stifled her temper and took in her surroundings.

Ostlers, maids, and various other servants rushed about

with horses, buckets, and packages that were presumably awaiting the mail coach.

So many people! A world of unfamiliarity.

A tremor ran through her.

"Are you ill?" He sounded more irritated than concerned.

She was miles from home, her sister, mother, and even the father she hated. She had less than a pound in her reticule and only one change of clothing. And yet, the urge to buy a ticket on the mail coach and travel anywhere away from here was a strong one.

But where could she go? Her father... he'd never allow her to return.

She glanced up and nodded. She knew nothing of him, and he knew nothing of her. It was imperative she remain optimistic. Perhaps she and her husband could find a way to get along without hating one another. She suspected not all marriages were like her parents' had been.

She hoped so, anyhow.

As far back as she could remember, she'd been an annoyance to her father. She did not relish the idea of being a burden and annoyance to her husband for the remainder of her life—or of his, whichever the case may be.

She did not relish the idea of having a husband that she feared. Fear was exhausting.

Her father treated her mother as though he hated her, and her mother kowtowed to his every whim. She knew this could not be the situation for all married couples, but it was hard to believe her own could be any different.

Especially after starting out in the manner that it had.

With a flick of her eyes, she stole a glance at his rugged features. His was not the face of a happily newlywed gentleman anticipating his wedding night. Rather more that of a man who was headed for the gallows.

Delightful.

THREE HOURS LATER, Lila stared out the window at the still-bustling yard. Much like waves rolling in and out, coaches, horses, and all manner of vehicle came and went even though night had fallen.

When she'd asked her husband if they were to dine privately, he'd scowled in her direction and informed her she could take her meal in their chamber. He'd be taking his downstairs with an ale or two.

She'd not seen him since.

Why didn't he talk to her? Already she missed Arianna's incessant stories, and even Fran's chattering about the most recent letter she'd received.

He'd only rented one room for the two of them. Every five minutes or so, her eyes drifted to the large bed that sat in the center of it.

Without even a cursory knock, the door opened, causing Lila to sit up straight. She had long ago changed into her night rail and dressing gown. She'd brushed out her hair and braided it.

She thought she was ready, but the sight of his tall and strapping form made the room feel considerably smaller. He removed his jacket before bothering to even look at her.

"The evening meal was to your satisfaction?" And then his gaze flickered to her half-eaten tray of food.

She nodded. "Yes. Thank you."

He walked to the washbasin and splashed some of the water onto his face.

"Is it always so loud here?" she asked him. Any sort of conversation would be better than this brooding silence he'd displayed all day.

"Quieter in back, but this was all they had available." With his back to her, he spoke somewhat defensively.

"I wasn't complaining." Lila hugged her knees into her chest and curled her bare toes around the edge of her chair. "Um. So…"

She lost track of what she was going to ask him when he dragged his shirt out of his breeches and then lifted it over his head.

Once, when she'd been reading one of Arianna's stories up in the loft of her father's stable at their southern estate, the stable master, after coming in from a ghastly thunderstorm, had disrobed right out in the open.

She'd stayed hidden and watched.

The stable master had been well into his fifties, though, and had a large paunch around his midsection.

Her husband…

She swallowed hard.

Seeing him thusly did little to calm her nerves. He had not an ounce of fat on him. His white skin stretched tightly over an abundance of sinewy muscles, making her wonder how he'd spent most of his life. Doing hard labor, she imagined.

"I didn't know dukes could look like you."

He stilled at her words but then turned to study her. "And how is that?" His jaw clenched. "Unrefined? Crude?"

"Oh, no! You must think very poorly of me to think I'd develop such an unfair opinion of anyone." It was her turn to frown. "You look…" Her gaze dragged unwittingly over his chest and abdomen. "Strong. I've never seen a duke that looked even remotely like you. They are usually very slim, effeminate almost. Except for my former fiancé, and he was only an earl when we were betrothed." And then she covered her mouth with her hand.

Did he know she'd been thrown over already?

Would he care? Most noblemen most definitely would consider her damaged goods.

Apparently, the Duke of Pemberth wasn't like most noblemen.

"What should I call you?" She could hardly imagine herself calling him Your Grace.

"The title is Pemberth," he responded but then ran one hand through his hair. "And you?

Lila took a deep breath. He was talking to her. After being married for nearly twelve hours, he was finally talking to her.

"Will you call me Lila? When we are alone, anyhow. I could hardly abide by you calling me Your Grace when we…" And then her gaze unwittingly drifted to the bed. "When no one else is present." And then she added, "My sister calls me Lila. Do you have any sisters? Or brothers perhaps? Won't you sit? Please?"

At last, an opportunity to learn something about him.

"No." But he sat down.

"Oh." She was rather disappointed at that. She'd hope for some friendly company. "Your estate, Glenn Abby? Do any other relatives live there with you? An aunt? A grandmother?" Or was it to be just the two of them?

"No."

He was doing it again. That not talking thing. She needed to ask him something that would require more than just a yes or no answer.

"Why did you marry me?" The question escaped before she could think it over properly. She wasn't usually one to babble but he... made her nervous.

He hadn't given her his full attention, in truth, up until that moment. He'd stared at the floor. Out the window.

Finally, his ice-cold blue eyes focused on her. "Why did *you* marry *me*?" His rejoining question surprised her. "Were you so determined that you should gain the title of 'duchess?'"

The question ought to have offended her, but she waved one hand through the air. "That is all my father. And I only married you because he insisted." Not a flattering answer, but... She raised her shoulders in a shrug. "Do I look as though I'm enamored with your title?"

He shrugged, but then dragged his gaze over her. "Oddly enough, no. Do you always do what your father tells you?" He finally seemed truly interested in something she might have to say.

Again, she shrugged. "I learned at a young age that to do anything other than his will resulted in... unpleasantness."

He continued staring at her. "You fear him?"

It was her turn to look elsewhere. Yes, she feared him. Her father had made a great deal of money from investments and... other business dealings. He was also born an earl. He had power. Not only over her but the people he'd surrounded them with.

She shrugged for a third time, this time without answering.

"Do you fear *me*?" His question was straightforward.

Lila hugged her knees even more tightly against her chest. "I've no reason to, have I?" Except that as his wife, she was his possession. "I am..." She licked her lips, her mouth suddenly quite dry. "I am hopeful that I will have no need to."

And then she lifted her chin, awaiting his next move.

VINCENT HAD DONE his best to pretend all day long that he had not just encumbered himself with a wife.

He could pretend all he wanted, but that did nothing to change the reality sitting across from him covered from neck to toe in a heavy dressing gown and night rail. His wife was a small woman who looked younger than her age. Long lashes framed rather pretty blue eyes and practically perfect features.

She'd admitted that she'd married him because she had been given no choice. She said she had not cared about a lofty title.

Oddly enough, he believed her.

"You have no need to fear me." His voice sounded gruffer than usual. But he meant it. The memory of her father violently removing her shawl and then tearing pins from her hair... Hell, what must she be expecting of him? "I won't force myself on you."

He wasn't so desperate that he'd ever force a woman—not even his wife.

"I am more than willing to lie with you." She did not blink as she spoke the words. Likely the notion of duty had been beaten into her.

He shook his head. He'd rather not bed a martyr.

But then she added, "I *want* to lie with you." This time, her eyes flared. He could almost imagine the blue of her gaze as a blue flame.

"You don't have to do this."

"Perhaps not for the reasons people choose to lie together, but…" Her gaze dropped to where his hands rested on his thighs. "If you change your mind, if you decide to send me back… My father… I was betrothed before and the gentleman… cried off. If I fail in this…" She lifted her chin to meet his eyes again. "I want you to lie with me."

Vincent drew in one long breath and then slowly released it.

Damn, Keenan.

"Do you not wish to lie with me?" Her brows furrowed. "Is it me in particular?" And then her eyes widened. "Do you not find women—"

"I find women quite nicely, thank you," he groused.

"Then why…?"

"Did I say I did not wish to lie with you?"

There, that put an end to her impertinent questions. She shook her head slowly. "I didn't mean to jump to conclusions."

If he'd thought he would be having such a conversation when he awoke this morning, he would have laughed outright at himself.

His wife of not even one day, who had been forced into marriage with him, was trying to talk him into bedding her. And for the first time all day, his sense of humor jumped to life.

As did his cock.

His gaze landed on her lips.

"So, you will?" she pleaded.

Vincent cleared his throat. Not exactly the scenario he'd envisioned for his wedding night. If he had envisioned one at all.

"If it is your wish."

"Oh, yes." She lowered her feet to the floor and leaned forward. "Now?"

He went to speak but only a choking sound emerged, causing him to groan a little and then scrub one hand down his face. "I don't imagine you've any experience." He half wished that she did. Although that would then mean… Nonetheless, it would make all of this so much easier.

She sat up straight at his question. "Of course not!"

How did a person go about this in such a dispassionate manner?

And yet, he realized he did not feel dispassionately when he looked at her. He'd found himself attracted to her since she'd glared at him just before the ceremony. It was her own practical approach that gave him pause.

She rose and smoothed her night rail down her hips and thighs. A lantern burned behind her, revealing curves he'd discovered when she'd fallen out of the carriage onto him earlier.

No, he was not the one who would experience any difficulty.

But she was a small woman. She was a virgin.

And he was… none of those things.

"Should I get on the bed, then?" She might as well have been asking him if he'd prefer mutton or beef.

"I suppose," he muttered. "No. Wait."

She paused and stared at him in some confusion. Vincent could not do this the same as he would repair a fence post or round up a herd.

He'd had some ale with his meal but suddenly wished he'd downed a few drams of whiskey. Pushing such thoughts away, he rose and crossed the room so that he stood directly in front of her. At least he'd washed the dirt and sweat off himself from his day's exertions.

She tilted her head back sharply just to meet his gaze.

"It will make it easier for you." His voice sounded gruff... gravelly. "If you are prepared."

With a determined glint in her eyes, she nodded. "Yes. Yes. That would be best." And then that furrowed brow of hers appeared again. "What does that require?"

"I should... you ought to... Oh, hell—" He reached one arm down to curve around her waist and dragged her body up against his.

God, but she felt fragile.

He lowered his mouth and claimed her lips.

She initially stiffened and went to draw back her head, but Vincent followed her hungrily, unwilling to draw out this dialogue any further.

If she didn't like it, he would stop. But she needed to have a taste of what was to come if she intended him to swive her that night.

Drawing his tongue along the seam of her lips, satisfaction rolled through him when she relaxed hers, allowing him entry. She tasted of something sweet, warm, and clean.

He'd gone too long without this... since before Keenan's death.

With a surge of excitement, he tightened his grip around her and when she made no sounds of protest, reached his hands beneath her knees, lifted her easily, and carried her to the bed.

A NEW EXPERIENCE

*P*lanning for such a life-altering event had not been easy, as sheltered and isolated as Lila had been throughout her life. She'd managed to ask Fran a few questions, and one of the housemaids, Dora, had been quite forthcoming, but nothing she'd learned on her own had prepared her for the magnitude of the actual experience itself.

All she could do when Pemberth claimed her mouth and then lifted her easily and carried her across the room was cling to him for dear life.

Dora had not mentioned anything about his tongue... doing these things. And although she might have thought the sensation would be unpleasant, Lila found it all rather intriguing.

In fact, she felt somewhat bereft when he dropped her onto the bed, forcing their mouths to disengage.

Most likely, he'd unfasten his breeches now.

"Do you want to extinguish the lantern?" She stared up at him.

His hands were indeed working at his waist. He did not answer her. He merely shook his head.

So, she would see it. It could not be very large, because Lila couldn't imagine…

Perhaps she'd rather not actually *see it*.

Laying back, she slid her feet apart, creating what she hoped would be an appropriate amount of room for him to work, and closed her eyes tightly.

She was not sure exactly what she had been waiting for, but when nothing happened, she opened her eyes and found him lying sideways on the bed, staring at her with his head resting on one hand.

And then she felt… *it*.

Glancing down was enough to confirm her suspicions. He had removed his breaches and—

Yes. The solid poking feeling at her side was indeed his member pressing into her. She just as quickly flicked her gaze back up to his face.

"Lila." For the first time since meeting him that morning, she sensed he might possibly be capable of smiling. Not that he was smiling at her now, but something danced in the back of those silver-blue eyes. "Are you certain you are prepared to do this?"

"Yes." She didn't want to take any chances. "Just do what you need to do." She closed her eyes again.

Then his hand was running down the length of her arm. He took a moment to draw a few light circles on the back of her hand and then moved his to rest on her abdomen.

Butterflies seemed to dance under her skin where he touched her. Her breath hitched when that same hand crept upward to just beneath her breast, cupping it from below.

"I won't hurt you, Lila." His voice sounded gravelly beside her ear.

She nodded slightly. Did she trust him?

Oddly enough, she did.

And then his fingers were slowly massaging the flesh that surrounded the tip. Pangs of... something hot coursed from where he touched her, to her center. Abandoning her earlier position, she squeezed her legs together and bent her knees. A tight pinch from his fingers had her swallowing hard.

When something warm and wet settled over her other breast, her eyes flew open.

She could only see the top of his head. He'd taken her nipple into his mouth, the fabric of her night rail no deterrent at all!

Awareness of a throbbing warmth between her legs replaced her initial shock and a moaning sound filled her ears.

Was that her?

It was! She squirmed, suddenly uncomfortable and wanting and scared all at the same time.

"I'm preparing you," he mumbled before claiming her lips with his again.

Again, she could only nod, as his lips chased around the sides of her mouth, trailing down to her earlobes.

She shivered, and his tongue swirled around the shell of her ear.

His hand had abandoned her breast and now caressed her thigh. She'd not even noticed that he'd lifted her night rail.

Part of her wanted to stop him, and the image of his member burned on the back of her eyelids, but she'd determined long ago the necessity of assuring her marriage could never be contested.

She knew her father all too well—his dishonesty and cheating—his nefariousness knew no bounds.

Pemberth's hand moved to the small mound just above her apex and all thoughts of her father fled. Dora had hinted at some of this, but Lila had not really believed her. Hunger grew inside of her.

Of their own volition, her hips thrust forward, inexplicably demanding more of his touch.

Ah, yes. Whereas before she'd been unable to even imagine him putting something inside of her there, she now wanted something...

She wanted anything.

She found herself twisting, writhing to be closer to him. And then his fingers slid into her folds, rubbing, circling, almost robbing her of her breath.

"How?" she panted. "What is—?" But then his mouth was devouring hers again. And just as his tongue thrust past her lips, one of his fingers slid inside of her.

His tongue thrust around her teeth and then deeper, just as he did with his hand. Another finger entered her and all she could do was clutch at him. Part of her felt like crying, part of her felt like screaming. This overwhelming onslaught was nearly too much.

VINCENT HADN'T EXPECTED to find himself straining against his own needs. He wasn't a rutting schoolboy.

But, by God, watching her come alive beneath his hand

—feeling her body tremble and reach for completion—had him struggling not to spend atop the bedclothes.

"So wet. So warm." He hadn't known he was speaking until he heard his own voice out loud. His hand caressed and then massaged around her opening before slipping a middle finger inside. She lifted and bucked beneath him in a haze of passion. But he enjoyed being in control and slowed her by leaning forward, pinning her down with his body.

When she cried out, he captured her sounds inside his own mouth.

Such a fine line between exquisite pleasure and torture.

Unable to wait one second longer, Vincent withdrew his hand and rested his arms along her head. He had never taken a virgin before.

Spreading her thighs wide with his knees, he settled atop her and pressed his tip against her soft opening.

Sensing her arousal, experiencing a hint of her tight, wet heat, his own excitement had him surging forward with one single thrust. There was nothing to do but to break her barrier; better not to prolong the process.

Ah, the exquisite pleasure.

Except the breathy panting sounds tickling his face were immediately replaced by a sharp gasp of pain. She stiffened beneath him, stilling his motions.

"Blast." He froze and hovered.

He'd taken her too quickly. He wasn't so oblivious as that. What if he were to move again? Should he pull back? It might cause her more pain.

Guilt hit him when he opened his eyes and saw tears rolling down the sides of her face onto the pillow. "Lila," he whispered, feeling as though he ought to call her by her title. Place 'Lady' before it at the very least. "Are you all right?" He began pulling away, but her hands clutched at him tightly.

Okay. No moving.

"Lila?" he asked again.

Her lashes fluttered and then eyes the color of the ocean on a sunny day gazed up at him.

She did not appear to be devastated or tortured. Although the tears continued to fall, she smiled. And then laughed. "That was it, was it not?"

What was what?

"We have done it?" she clarified.

Which nearly had him laughing. Instead, he merely nodded. "Your father cannot charge me with failure to consummate." The words were so ridiculous, and her relief so obvious, that he couldn't help but smile back at her.

But there was more. So much more. He held himself in check so that she could grow used to his intrusion.

"I'm going to begin moving again." He stared at her lips, swollen from his kisses, and then back into her eyes. His own need demanded he get back to business.

She nodded. "But," her voice caught him just as he went to pull back, "slowly?"

In answer, he captured her lips again and slowly slid his tongue past her teeth once.

And then again.

She nodded.

He pulled back less than an inch and then crept forward again. She did not close her eyes this time, and neither did he. He would watch her, follow her signals as he gradually increased the depth and pace of his strokes.

Her eyelids grew heavy, and Vincent could hold back no longer.

He reached for her hands and lifted them to the bedframe. "Place your hands here." He wrapped her fingers around the cool metal.

He'd not had a woman in nearly four months. She was his wife.

She was his.

He'd all but bought and paid for her.

Frantic with lust, Vincent finally allowed his cock free rein, driving and shoving himself to completion. Just before he was about to spend, she convulsed and cried out.

Deeper. Again deeper.

His release came in an explosion of red and white light. He emptied himself inside of her, prodded one last time, and then collapsed as though boneless.

LILA EDGED herself out from beneath the hulk of a man who slept atop her, dislodging his member in the process. She felt sticky, shaky, and not at all certain that any of that had been what she'd expected.

Some aspects had been so very tender and sweet, and then others had seemed almost violent. In the light of the lantern, she stared at him and wondered who he was. His skin shone almost golden, shadows and ridges creating a myriad of swirls over his skin.

Sliding her feet to the floor, she winced. Blood and... something else. His seed. No maid would ever discover these sheets. In the morning, Lila would change them out for one she'd stuffed into her bag.

She'd have evidence. Just in case.

She could not trust her father.

As she stood, her muscles protested, and twinges from between her legs reminded her that she was no longer a maiden.

She had... enjoyed it. Even when he'd seemed more animal than man.

When he'd placed her hands upon the bars, she'd felt a moment of fear. But after that, she'd been grateful for something to hold her steady so that she could take him deeper and reach for him with... she didn't quite know.

But in the end, she could not deny her reaction to what they shared.

Not at all what she'd expected.

She tiptoed across to the tray of food she'd barely touched earlier and broke off a piece of bread. Dropping to the hard wooden chair, she bit into it enthusiastically.

Now that it was over, her appetite had returned.

Would he sleep through the night like that? Wearing nothing?

He was quite handsome. In all her imaginings, she'd never suspected her husband would look like him. Her initial fiancé, although handsome and well-built, had been dark and not nearly as large.

Pemberth was large.

All of him.

It had fit. He'd driven it in and out of her—that pulsing staff of rigid flesh.

At first, it had seemed as though it would not fit, but then her body had adjusted... made room for him.

And it had only hurt in those first few moments. After that, she'd felt it deep inside and she'd known a...

Knowing.

A belonging.

She took another bite of the bread but slowed her chewing when he moaned and rolled over, exposing himself to her in the dim light. She'd known it wasn't always erect but was still slightly surprised at the shriveled creature it had become.

Lila obviously had a great deal to learn.

"Are you well?" She'd been so intent upon the change in him that she'd not realized he was awake.

Forcing herself to meet his gaze, she nodded.

"I did not hurt you?"

"Only a little." She rose from her chair, wet a cloth, and crossed the room to hand it to him. "Do you mind if I change the sheet?"

He'd taken the cloth without question but then glanced up curiously. He looked different to her but she wondered if it was her imagination. His lips seemed fuller, and she noticed tiny little lines at the sides of his eyes, as though he'd spent either a good deal of time out of doors or that he did, in fact, laugh.

She hoped it was the latter. "There is more bread and butter." Perhaps he'd worked up an appetite as well. "And some cheese... if you like." How was it that he was a stranger, and yet...?

"I didn't hate it." She would try to break through some of this awkwardness. "I thought I would, but I didn't."

The man seemed to have not one iota of modesty. She'd expected that he would don his breeches once again and perhaps pull on his shirt, but he'd simply crossed to the tray and taken the seat she'd vacated.

Stark naked.

Although he'd pulled her gown over halfway up her body, he'd never removed it from her completely. A few damp spots darkened the material in some embarrassing locations.

Around the bodice of the night rail and lower, where some of his seed had dripped.

"I'm glad." He spoke around the cheese he'd taken a bite of. And then an almost smile. "I did not hate it either."

Something in his look had heat rushing up her neck. What did a lady say in response to any of this? Did it matter, since she was his wife? Somehow, she didn't think she could offend him in any way.

He was unlike any noblemen she'd ever been acquainted with.

"How long have you been duke?"

His almost-smile disappeared completely, and his mouth set into a grim line. "Three months."

"I'm sorry." Had his father been ill? Had it been sudden? That would explain his morose countenance. "Were you close to your father?"

He tossed the hunk of cheese he'd been eating back onto the tray. "My father died over twenty years ago. My older brother held the title."

Lila had removed the sheet and was opening the much finer quality linen she'd removed from her bag. Without needing to be asked, he crossed to the other side of the bed and assisted her. Despite the nature of their conversation, she couldn't help enjoying watching his muscles flex and strain beneath his skin.

"I'm sorry," Lila said again. "Was he ill?" Her curiosity got the better of her.

"No." Tight-lipped, he stuffed the linen beneath the mattress. "We'd best get some rest. I'd like to arrive at Glenn Abby before nightfall tomorrow. To do so, we'll have to get an early start." He'd thrown the patched counterpane back onto the mattress and, without consulting her, extinguished the lantern.

Lila climbed back under the blanket, careful to give him more than half of the bed.

Overall, her marriage was a success.

Her next objective: lower his defenses. After that, she could ask him about sending for Arianna.

A WIFE IN TRUTH

*L*ila opened her eyes to a room that was not her own.

This ceiling was much lower, cracked in several places and a dingy ivory. No large carved posts, no rose-colored velvet drapes.

The realization of Lila's new life dawned on her slowly.

And yet, she realized as she turned her head, she had awoken alone.

She was no longer a maiden. After six and twenty years, she'd finally given herself to a man, to her husband.

Who was likely already growing impatient that she'd yet to have risen for the day. Lila glanced toward the bag she'd brought along with her. She should have removed the gown she'd intended to wear today and laid it out so it would not be wrinkled. She ought to have brushed out the one she'd worn the day before. Things Fran normally did but Lila had taken for granted. She'd have to remember to thank her maid when she saw her again.

She'd not slept a great deal, far too aware of the man

dozing beside her and today she would pay for her lack of sleep.

Without a maid to assist her.

Lazy. She chastised herself and climbed out of bed to tackle the business of dressing and preparing for another day's travel.

When she finally presented herself outside, she was disappointed to see that her husband had saddled his mount, leaving Lila to ride inside the coach alone again. She'd rather hoped to have some company today.

She'd hoped he might seem friendlier.

Catching sight of her, he nodded in approval, handed the mare off to a driver and covered the distance between them. "You're prepared to travel?" His gaze flicked to her bag. "Did you get anything to eat?"

She shook her head. She normally wasn't very hungry in the mornings.

"Calvin!" He waved a hand to the manservants who rode up with the driver. "Her Grace requires some rations to break her fast."

The day before, Lila hadn't paid much heed to anything or anyone, she'd been so fraught with uncertainty. Today she took note of both the driver and the outrider. Both were similar in appearance, red-haired and burly. The driver, whom she remembered being addressed as Drake, appeared to be the elder of the two. Perhaps they were brothers.

"I don't normally eat much in the mornings." Suddenly, she felt shy again. She might not have this chance again, however, anytime soon. "I was hoping you would ride with me today." And then she bit her lip.

With a glance over his shoulder, he studied his mount.

And then his eyes shifted back to the carriage. "I usually ride."

"But we are newly married. I would like to come to know more about my husband." And for some reason, she felt herself blushing again.

Lila was not one to blush. She wondered when all of these unsettling emotions might settle down. Surely, they couldn't last throughout the course of her marriage.

Pemberth glanced over his shoulder again. Calvin was already emerging from the inn, a small basket in hand.

And then Pemberth surprised and pleased her. "Very well. For a while, anyhow."

Excusing himself, he went to have a word with his outrider, took the basket from him, and returned to assist Lila into the carriage.

If she was to endure another day in this Godforsaken vehicle, at least she would have company while doing so. She sat facing forward and her husband climbed in beside her.

The interior shrunk with his presence, and Lila's heart felt as though it skipped every other beat. Hopefully, this hadn't been a mistake.

As the carriage lurched into motion, Lila gripped the leather strap and turned herself to partially face him.

He didn't look at all comfortable. The bench seat hadn't been built for a man of his size, and she ought to have perhaps considered this before posing her request. Irritating him was not going to get him to send for Arianna any sooner.

"I'm glad it isn't raining," she began. Anything to fill the long silences he seemed to prefer. "You mentioned you were needed back at your estate. Do you have meetings?"

Oh, but his eyes were such a light blue that they almost appeared silver. He shifted on the bench and turned to face her as well. He'd lifted one knee partially onto the upholstery, causing their knees to touch.

Lila swallowed hard.

"No," he answered curtly.

"Tell me about the duties that fill your time." She played with the ruffle on one of her sleeves. Perhaps she appeared less attractive to him today. She'd been unable to affect the same neat chignon Fran had the day before and the pale blue traveling gown she'd donned was more wrinkled than smooth.

He drew her attention back to his face when he let out a long sigh. "The Pemberth Dukedom. My estate." And then, "*Our* estate." He met her gaze steadily. "Is… not financially viable at this time. Tenants are quickly abandoning it for more lucrative prospects."

Lila processed such information. "So, my father did not pay you to marry me?"

He was shaking his head. "He did not." His answer came as a surprise. "I married you in order to pay off a debt. A debt incurred by my brother."

For some reason, this information deflated Lila more than she would have imagined. Had her father paid him to marry her, then he would have had some choice in the matter.

Had the debt been his own, he would have still had some choice in the matter.

But he'd had no choice at all.

A gun might as well have been held to his head when he'd taken his wedding vows.

⁓

VINCENT COULD SEE she'd been unsuspecting of the true nature of their marriage. Although she'd been partially right, he supposed there were, indeed, some differences.

She looked almost disappointed.

"I am even more of a burden than I had imagined." Her sunny outlook seemed to have vanished and some of the light left her eyes. Vincent didn't know why it mattered. He hadn't expected his wife's emotions to affect him much at all.

But…

"I needed to marry anyhow." Which was true, of course. And she had satisfied him immensely the night before. He reached out a hand and touched her knee in a few soothing strokes. "You are as good as any other."

Perhaps he ought to have phrased that differently.

"I mean—"

"No, I understand. It's better than the last time. At least you did not marry a spinster to spite him."

Vincent shifted in search of a more comfortable position. "Is this damn carriage hitting every rock and rut in all of England?"

She didn't answer him, choosing instead to turn away and stare out the window. He felt like something of a jackass for speaking his mind so plainly.

"You mentioned you were betrothed before." Quimbly had been upfront about this fact but hadn't explained why she'd been jilted. It had worried Vincent at the time but now, having seen her, he couldn't imagine why the man had done something so dishonorable as to cry off and leave a perfectly fine young woman to suffer the consequences.

Especially her. His cock stirred at the memory of the night before. He couldn't remember ever getting so excited over any woman. Perhaps it was the novelty of having her for a wife…

"I've convinced myself that Blakely was more reluctant to take on my father as an in-law than he was to take me on as a wife," she answered without turning around. "My former fiancé married another before breaking it off. There are rumors…" But then she shuttered her gaze. "Both of our fathers tried to force Lord Blakely to honor the betrothal but, rather than do so, he eloped with another woman."

"Gretna?"

"Yes. I've never seen her, but my father says she's hideous. Blakely is the heir to the Duke of Waters and, I'm told, chose to marry Miss Emily Goodnight, a bespectacled bluestocking, rather than be saddled with me."

Vincent rubbed his chin. "Definitely the father-in-law." He slid her a sideways glance, hoping to lift her spirits. "His loss is my gain."

"Ha!" She turned skeptical eyes back on him, ignoring the window once again.

Ah, yes. "As of last evening, I'm quite pleased to find myself saddled with you." He allowed his gaze to rove down her neck, to her chest and waist. The fingers on his hand that remained on her leg began gradually gathering the material of her skirt, edging it upward.

Her breath hitched.

"Is it wise?" She took a guess at his intent. "To do it again so soon?"

This gave him pause.

"Are you sore?" She hadn't acted as though she was tender, but how was he to know?

She shook her head, eyes wide, but then answered, "A little."

"There are other things a man and woman can do." They had a long distance to travel today with nothing for entertainment. The uncomfortable seats would make sleep nigh impossible.

His fingers renewed their purpose, exposing toned calves hidden beneath woolen stockings. And above them, the softer and naked flesh of her thigh. In less than two minutes, he managed to have her sitting in a pile of her skirts, both lovely legs exposed for his enjoyment.

"May I?" he asked with a cock of one eyebrow. She frowned in confusion but nodded.

Later, he'd examine how she'd come to trust him so easily, but for now, he dropped onto the floor, kneeling before her. Small white teeth tugged at her bottom lip, sending what blood remained in his head to a much lower part of his anatomy.

Using both hands now, he pushed her skirts higher.

He'd not seen her last night. None of her, really. He'd touched her intimately, he'd driven his body into hers, but he'd not been able to enjoy her this way.

"Lie back," he ordered and as she did so, he lifted her knees and set each upon one of his shoulders.

Lush and pink, better than he'd imagined. She let out a cry, and he halted to meet her gaze. "A woman can be beautiful in more ways than one." As he spoke, his hand slid upward. He could not resist.

He leaned forward and stole the most intimate of kisses.

~

WHEN LILA HAD SET out to get to know the man she'd married a little better, in all her imaginings, she'd not imagined…

This.

One hand on the strap above her, her other searched for purchase on the bench. She'd nearly slid off the seat and her knees dangled over his shoulders. Feeling like something of a voyeur to her own illicit behavior, she drank in the sight of his thick blond hair as he worked between her thighs.

Dora had not even hinted at such… depravity.

The carriage hit a rut and his grip tightened when her hips slid, pressing her harder against his…

Mouth.

"Oh." She couldn't stop herself from crying out as the friction of the stubble on his face rubbed against her. And then the warmth of his tongue. The wetness added to her own.

A trembling need was building inside her, the same one she recognized from the night before. Only this time, the pleasure might be absent any pain.

She writhed as he created sensations she could hardly begin to comprehend. What on earth was he doing to insight them? Merely contemplating where his tongue was, that he enjoyed doing something like this, made her want to thrust herself at him harder.

His wanting her made her want him.

"Pemberth!" His name escaped on a gasp.

His hand covered her mouth, stifling her sounds.

"If you make too much noise, Drake will think we want him to stop." His voice was muffled but she appreciated that he hadn't paused in his activities.

And now she tasted the salt on his hand. He'd been touching her.

And it didn't matter. Nothing mattered but this. By now the jostling of the carriage only heightened each stroke of his tongue, each thrust of his fingers. The world spiraled around her as she gave herself over completely. He could play her. He could dine on her. This need... it had stolen her will in the most unexpected way.

And just as the world shattered, she became vaguely aware of the carriage listing to one side and slowing to a halt.

She slumped onto the bench with closed eyes, uncaring of her modesty or what was going on around them.

"That damned wheel!" Her husband's voice penetrated her satiated fog, and he drew back, leaving her feeling somewhat bereft all of a sudden.

The carriage. The wheel. A driver and an outrider right outside the door.

"Oh, blast." She lowered her gown and sat up primly on the bench. Pemberth's lips were glossy and his face slightly damp.

Feeling rather proud of herself, she handed him a clean cotton handkerchief.

The broken carriage had irritated him, yes, but not so much that he didn't send her a wicked glance before opening the door and leaping out.

A NEW HOME

*P*emberth had been correct—the back-left wheel had cracked right through. It wasn't raining, or snowing, but what with Christmas just a few weeks away, winter was in the air. Lila located a conveniently placed boulder and sat huddled in her coat as the man who'd had his face between her legs a mere thirty minutes earlier lay on his back beneath the worn-out carriage, pounding and twisting at the broken wheel.

Her gaze remained fixed upon the muscles in his thighs and... higher. It was difficult to feel any sort of irritation at their delay after he'd just so recently and thoroughly... prepared her.

"Hand me that wrench, will you?"

Drake stepped forward and placed some sort of tool in Pemberth's outstretched hand and then peered down to examine his employer's handiwork. The driver had initially attempted to make the repair, but when he'd proven unsuccessful, Pemberth had not hesitated to crawl under the vehicle himself.

Calvin had ridden Pemberth's mount ahead, in search of another conveyance in case this one could not be made functional again.

"The other wheel looks like it could go just as easily." Her husband's muffled voice carried out from beneath the coach. Lila sighed, remembering how it had felt when that same voice had been muffled by—

"But this ought to do it." And then he was rolling out, his shirt covered in dirt and his hair looking even wilder than when it had been between her— "But we'll have to take it slow."

And then he was off the ground and offering her his hand. "Your carriage awaits."

Vincent teased her but she also sensed him withdrawing once again. She wasn't overly concerned this time. As little time as they'd spent together, she was beginning to feel as though she could know him.

He assisted her into the carriage, disappeared, she presumed to make sure they returned all the tools to the boot, and then returned just a few minutes later. She didn't care that he was sweaty and covered with dust and grime from working beneath the vehicle.

She couldn't help feeling more physically drawn to him than she had last night. This time, when the carriage began moving, it creaked along very slowly. The slower pace meant they'd be traveling longer but it did, however, cut down on some of the jostling and bouncing.

"Do you think we'll have to stop again?"

He leaned back, stretching his legs across so that his feet could rest on the backward-facing bench, and closed his eyes. "This length of road is pretty isolated. No inns that I can remember. If Calvin finds anything, we'll meet him along the way."

"And if he doesn't?" Lila couldn't help asking.

"He'll meet us at Glenn Abbey."

He'd said he only inherited three months ago. "Have you lived there all your life?"

He nodded.

"Was your brother married?"

"Nope."

Oh, they were back to this again. "You said tenants were leaving. Is this a recent phenomenon?"

"Define recent." Ah, two words from him this time.

"Within the last, say, three months?" She risked souring his mood again, but she was curious about their circumstances.

"Yes." He shifted then, raised one arm and tugged her so that she laid against him rather than the wall of the coach. "Are you done interrogating me yet?"

"You would do the same." Although she did not appreciate his arrogant attitude, she did like the feeling of his arm around her, and the solid comfort of his chest and side. "If you were me."

With him holding her, instead of feeling every rut the carriage drove over, she felt the gentle swell and dip of each breath he took. After riding some distance in silence, he inhaled deeply.

"I am not much of a businessman, as my brother was. We're already in financial straits, and they fear I won't be able to pull us out." A long exhale. "And they're right to do so. You're on the bad end of a sorry bargain, Lila Saint-Pierre."

Lila absorbed his words rather than respond right away.

He'd known well enough how to deal with her father. His servants obviously respected him.

He'd fixed the carriage wheel, for heaven's sake, something she doubted her father or even Lord Blakely ever would have been able to accomplish.

"You seem smart enough to me." And of course, this only drew silence from him. "Tell me where you feel your intelligence is lacking."

He groaned.

"You don't have to if you don't wish, but I will only keep asking until you do."

Was that a kiss he'd just pressed atop her head? She couldn't be certain and glanced up to see if she could read his expression. He met her eyes with a wry smile. "I did not attend university, as my brother did. The reports and accounts perplex me." He shook his head. "And I cannot hire someone else to handle such matters. They are my direct responsibility."

Lila raised one hand to his chest and rested it there. "Will there be many parties for me to attend?"

He stiffened, but she stroked her hand up and down until he seemed to relax again. "No parties to my knowledge. There is a small village nearby, of course. And the ladies in the village head up some sort of charities, as far as I know."

"I've only brought a few books to read. And I've never been all that accomplished at any particular musical instrument. When I tried painting my sister in watercolors, she nearly fell over for laughing so hard."

"Is there a point to this recitation of your ineptitudes? Are you already complaining that you will be bored at—"

"My father is a horrible person. A villain. It's possible

he's even a murderer." She'd never been certain of the latter, however. "But one thing my father has always excelled at is the running of his estates. Making money. And whenever he was away, I made it a point to understand his business. If you don't mind, I'd be more than willing to go over yours."

He didn't answer her immediately, but she was learning that this was his way. He thought before he spoke and said only that which was necessary.

"I will think about it." His voice rumbled under her ears.

She sat up and stared at him curiously. "I would not offer if I was not confident."

He wiggled his shoulders and shifted on the bench, as though something about her offer discomforted him. "We shall see."

Lila turned and rested her cheek against him once again. She had more work to do.

He must learn to trust her.

THE REMAINDER OF THE AFTERNOON, they'd pressed on diligently, stopping only twice on the side of the road so Pemberth could check the wheel and so she could stretch her legs.

She had not expected to enjoy getting to know this husband of hers, nor had she expected to feel so comfortable in his protective embrace.

He was a man who'd married her under duress.

Likely, these strange emotions had merely been stirred up by the exquisite sexual gratification he'd given her.

Twice.

Even the thought of that second time had her reaching for her fan.

It was as though her father, a man she'd hated for most of her life, a man she'd feared, had somehow handed her the perfect husband.

Who also made a most comfortable pillow.

Admittedly, he was not much of a talker, but she was gradually learning a little at a time. Feeling truly optimistic for the first time in her life, Lila snuggled deeper into her husband and dozed.

THE DARKNESS WOKE HER. And then the cessation of the bouncing and rocking she'd endured over the last few days.

She sat up from the bench she'd taken over completely only a moment before the door swung open and a tired-looking Pemberth peered inside.

"We're home," he announced.

Lila gathered her belongings and allowed him to assist her down the step. There wasn't much to see. It must be the middle of the night, but she could hear ocean waves crashing in the distance.

Most of her life, she'd been told her arrival as duchess would be honored by the servants standing at attention for inspection in lieu of a greeting. She would be wearing a fine gown and the household would be anxious for her arrival.

Her mother had told her all of this anyhow. Her father insisted it was their due.

As she stepped onto the gravel, though, she welcomed the quiet. She was cold and exhausted and only wanted to crawl into a warm bed so that she could fall back asleep.

With a few words to his servants, her husband took her bag from her and led her to the large front door.

The arched doorway was tall, at least three feet taller

than her husband even. She tilted her head back and only saw that the stonework reached high into the sky. The tower disappeared in the darkness.

Pemberth steered her forward and, if possible, it seemed even colder inside.

She glanced around in search of a housekeeper, or butler even.

"They're abed. They've too much work to do tomorrow for me to awaken them in the middle of the night." He seemed to have read her mind.

Lila nodded in understanding, still feeling a little dazed from being awakened in such unfamiliar surroundings.

"Did you ride on the box with Drake?" Calvin had taken his mount.

"Until the sun went down. We took turns walking ahead with a lantern."

She was coming to realize she appreciated this aspect of her husband. He was not unwilling to do anything he'd ask another to do for him.

But he was also the duke.

And she was the duchess.

They'd shared a bed the night before out of necessity. It had been a good start for them.

Pemberth struck a flint, lit a lantern set on a nearby table, and then gestured with it for her to precede him. As they climbed a narrow and winding staircase to the second floor, she wondered if he was taking her to a separate chamber than his, or if he would wish to keep her with him.

They reached the landing, and he turned to face her. "I haven't set up in the master's chamber yet. And yours hasn't been tended to since my mother's death, decades ago. If you'd prefer, I suppose we can wake Mrs. Smith to have a guest-chamber made up, but—"

"You are my husband, no? I will share yours." Sometimes her mouth functioned without her brain telling it to do so. "That is unless—"

"No." He gave her that almost-smile. She was learning his expressions so much that she recognized it even in the flickering shadows. "I've a large bed. I'd prefer to keep my wife with me."

Despite being practically asleep on her feet, an odd thrill ran down her spine.

They'd share this room for now, but in the back of her mind, she was already making a list of matters she would tend to.

One of the first would be to establish her and her husband in the ducal suites. This man had not completely embraced the title left to him by his brother.

She was the perfect person to help him do just that.

GLENN ABBEY

*L*ila had intended to get an early start the next morning but opened her eyes to see the sun already slanting in brightly. Her husband had held her through the night but not made any attempt to repeat what they'd done the night before... or even what he'd done in the carriage.

Lila had to admit she had been grateful for that.

He'd walked a great deal of the remainder of their journey. He must have been exhausted.

She rolled over and examined his chamber with the benefit of the full light of day.

A wardrobe. A desk.

Two windows, both with drapes that must be centuries old.

Sitting up, she dangled her feet over the edge of the tall bed. The carpet looked even older than the drapes.

Personal objects of her husband's lured her to lower her feet to the floor so that she could examine what he felt necessary, or precious enough, to keep close at hand.

She smiled at the strands of his curling blond hair left behind in a well-used brush. And at the razor and comb he left casually strewn atop his bureau. The thought struck her that he did not keep a valet.

Perhaps another item to add to her list.

Trailing to the desk, she sat down and picked up an unfinished document he'd been writing. Supplies to be purchased. Printed in an almost child-like script. A few other notes that she didn't understand about sheep in the third quarter... repairs.

She did not open the drawer.

On a small table beside the bed was a small jewel box. Inside, a ring with the same faded crest that had adorned the door of their carriage.

Why did he not wear his ducal ring?

Sounds at the door had her hastily replacing it and turning around.

"Fran!" It seemed as though a lifetime had passed since she'd seen her dearest maid and companion. She flew across the room into the older woman's arms and squeezed her with all her might.

"No tears, then? He has treated you kindly?" Fran stood back and examined her closely. "His Grace asked that I did not awaken you, but that I assist you in dressing so that he can show you about the estate."

"No tears." Lila sniffed. "And I believe he is a good man."

So far. Unless her instincts were wrong. He'd been kind.

He'd been more than kind.

He wanted to spend the day with her. Showing her the estate. Her new home! He was not going to turn back into the sullen stranger she married.

"There's a room across the way where he told me to unpack

61

your belongings. What kind of duke is he, that he doesn't have a proper chamber for his bride? Anyhow, come along with me, dearie, and I'll get you prepared for the day. You look as though a rat has been sleeping in your hair." Lila followed the energetic woman across the hall into the other room.

"We've a good deal of work to do," she told her cheerfully.

And for one of the first times in her life, she felt she might have something to offer this world.

∼

"COME IN." Vincent barely glanced up from the journal of transactions as he bid Calvin to enter.

Only it wasn't Calvin.

The first day, his wedding day, his wife had deliberately chosen unflattering garments in some rebellious gesture against her father or him or both of them. The second morning, his wife had dressed without the assistance of her maid.

Today, she appeared every inch a duchess.

So much so that he wondered how on earth he was going to manage to keep her satisfied. Two people could not spend all of their time in the bedchamber, after all.

She wore her silken strands of coffee-colored hair in a braided coronet wound about the top of her head. Her skin glowed and the vibrant azure gown she'd chosen matched her eyes almost perfectly.

Vincent awkwardly pushed back his chair so that he could rise. "Your Grace," he addressed her.

A secret light danced behind those eyes. Ah, she might

look the duchess, but this was the same woman he'd had writhing and bucking beneath his mouth the day before.

"*Your Grace.*" She dipped into a graceful curtsey.

For all of thirty seconds, Vincent seemed to lose track of any intelligent thought. He'd sent her maid up when he'd discovered the luggage coach had arrived early.

Ah, yes.

He cleared his throat. "Are you rested enough to see some of the estate today?"

She gave him a sideways smile. "I am, Your Grace."

His mouth twitched. "And have you broken your fast?"

Fluttering lashes. "I have." Her tongue peeked out from between plump vermillion lips. "Your Grace."

Was she flirting with him?

And then she seemed flustered. "If you'd rather, we could stay here and go over some of those reports."

He was inclined to believe the best of her, but he could not forget whose daughter she was.

And then she shrugged. "Or not."

"Tomorrow we will ride." And then. "Do you ride?"

"Of course. I can change if you'd prefer—"

"What you're wearing is beautiful." He did not want her to change. He cleared his throat. "I'd thought to give you a tour of the castle."

She'd seemed stunned by his compliment but managed to nod. "I would love to learn more about your family. Your history. Saint-Pierre?" She tilted her head with a smile. "I had not even considered my new name until you called me by it yesterday."

Vincent offered an arm and walked them to the door. He'd not considered that she knew very little about him.

About a man she now belonged to. She'd left her home, her family. "You were happy to see your maid?"

She gave him her smiles all too easily. "I was."

Although his legs were much longer than hers, he hardly had to slow his steps at all. She moved eagerly beside him.

"This is the formal drawing-room." Vincent opened a door and winced. The furniture appeared faded and worn. "I would suggest refurbishing it or replacing it all together but..." He would not refer to their empty pockets this morning.

"The windows are lovely." She released his arm to stroll slowly toward the center, just beneath an elaborate but dust-covered chandelier.

A duchess indeed. She stood in the middle of the room— a blaze of color set in a portrait painted using only black and whites. Watching her, he realized that the room was grand. If only...

He waited a moment and then closed the door behind her after they exited to the corridor once again.

"Did you love him?" He wasn't certain why he'd asked. But she had been betrothed for nearly two decades.

"My father?"

"No. The man who jilted you." Although he wondered that, too...

But she was shaking her head. "He was my... escape. I didn't know him, really. I was horribly disappointed to learn he'd married another lady. I had hoped... And then my father made all of us move from where I'd lived all my life. I didn't understand at the time, but I think perhaps he had no choice. It was as though he was... running." She pinched her lips together.

"Was it me, in particular, that you did not wish to marry? Is there someone else?"

Her eyes grew wide, as though the thought had just occurred to her. "No." And then she narrowed her eyes. "What of you?"

He shook his head.

There was no one in particular. He'd not courted any of the local landowners' daughters because he'd considered himself a sorry prospect, just as he'd told her. Keenan had been the prize.

"Tell me some of what you learned from spying on your father." He would call it what it was.

She stiffened beside him.

"I meant no insult. But that was what it was, was it not?"

"He kept us in the dark about anything that mattered."

"And what did you discover?" Would she tell him or were her loyalties still with her miscreant of a father?

They had arrived at a set of double doors and Vincent paused, awaiting her answer, before opening them.

"I learned that in order to turn a profit, estates must look beyond agriculture. There are various investments... Machinery is going to overtake the labor of many men." She stared at the floor, blushing almost, as she spoke such insight.

Vincent opened the doors in a sweeping gesture. The ballroom. Unused since his mother's death.

She peered inside, at the vast parquet floor set beneath sixteen different chandeliers. When she looked back at him, Vincent thrust his hands into his pockets.

"Perhaps you can take a look at our books once you've settled in."

"Our?"

In for a penny, in for a pound. "Ours."

~

"So this pile is correspondence and reports; this one is for receipts; this pile is...?"

"Unknown?" He winced as he said the word. It was the tallest stack by far.

After discovering his wife to be an accomplished horse-woman, they'd spent the past week riding over the estate and visiting tenants who had not yet decided to abandon him. The weather had been cold and crisp, but everywhere they went, they'd been invited inside for hot tea or coffee and to 'warm the wee duchess up.' The tenants loved her already.

As did his servants.

This morning, lazy flakes of snow had been falling from the sky and Vincent had convinced his energetic wife to remain inside while he met with his steward and three of his most stalwart tenants. Last year's crops had yielded less than the year before. They needed to make some decisions before proceeding into the next growing season. Vincent had heard of estates becoming more profitable by increasing herd sizes and focusing on maintaining greater land areas in order to support the demand.

He needed money to increase the herd sizes but would figure that out later. With larger herds, the future promised income from mutton, wool, and even some dairy products.

He'd also been wondering which of these machines Lila mentioned might increase efficiencies.

He'd returned from the vigorous discussion to find his

wife sitting at his brother's—nay—*his* desk, sorting through paperwork that he'd been avoiding for weeks now.

"Pemberth?" She pulled him back to the task at hand. "You did say you didn't mind."

He scrubbed one hand down his face in an attempt to wipe away his embarrassment. He hated the fact that something so seemingly benign had defeated him.

"I don't mind." He exhaled. "I'm just…" She trusted him with so much. Her security, her safety.

Her body.

The only night he had not bedded her had been the night of their arrival. They'd both been too exhausted.

And she was not shy. She'd enthusiastically agreed to almost anything he thought to suggest. And once… it had been she who had been creative.

And now she was making an attempt to unravel this mess he'd allowed to accumulate.

The swishing of her dress recaptured his attention as she rose and slowly moved around the desk. She surprised him then by wrapping her arms around his waist and squeezing. "My sister is one of the smartest people I know. She paints the most beautiful portraits using watercolors but give her a page of math problems to solve and she's like to pull her hair out." Vincent rested his chin atop his wife's elegantly braided coiffure. "I, on the other hand, enjoy such tasks. You are doing me a favor by allowing me to sort through such a puzzle."

"You needn't placate me this way to soothe my ego."

"What ego? You are the least arrogant man I've ever met."

Vincent shook his head. *Who is this woman?*

"You are a good man, Pemberth. And quite on the way to making an excellent duke."

At this, he laughed outright at her optimistic faith in him.

"You are a *good man*," she scolded. And then that smile of hers cracked open the seals on his heart. "Now, you're cold as ice. Sit by the fire and I'll see what I can do about deciphering your brother's handwriting." She released him and proceeded to rub her hands together as though anticipating a great meal. "This way, you'll be right here in case I have any questions."

Vincent had stopped on his way home to repair a section of fence. He hadn't realized until that moment how cold he'd become.

And as long as she might require his assistance... He lowered himself into the large wing-backed chair near the hearth, leaned back his head, and closed his eyes.

He listened as she efficiently sorted through one of the piles.

She'd told him she'd paid attention to her father's business dealings. Something he'd failed to do. He'd been more interested in learning about soil and animals and the people who worked the land.

"I believe you are correct about agriculture. Crop yields are diminishing annually." Vincent opened his eyes to stare at the fire. "Miller, Freddy, and Simon are open to moving toward planting more pasture and increasing the herds, but Helmsworth wants to wait."

"Helmsworth, he is your steward, correct? And the others... They have tenant houses." He'd introduced her to dozens of families over the past week, and yet, she remembered.

"Correct."

"What are his reasons?" Now she was flipping through the correspondence as though she was dealing cards.

"We need funds to increase the herd sizes. I was hoping to get a loan." The idea sounded outlandish to him as he spoke the words. Merely the fact that he would require a loan to accomplish something so simple was humiliating. And now he was telling his wife, no less.

"So we need money." She stated the fact baldly. "Not simply to refurbish the drawing-room."

Vincent nodded, still not looking at her.

"Very well. I'd best look hard at all of this, then. If anyone can find a source for revenue, it's the Earl of Quimbly's wayward daughter. Trust me."

Vincent let out a scoffing sound.

"Pemberth." Her voice demanded his full attention.

He turned his head to meet her serious gaze.

"If there is a possible way, I will discover it."

ESTATE DETAILS

*L*ila had never imagined she could find so much satisfaction in her daily routine as a wife.

In the mornings, she and Pemberth went riding, visiting various farmers and tenants in the area, and if the weather did not permit, sometimes explored secret nooks and crannies inside the estate. They shared a nuncheon and went their separate ways for the afternoon—he attended to fences and horses and sheep and whatnot, and she continued reading through the documents that had accumulated over the past two years.

The former duke, Keenan—she had come to feel almost as though she knew him—had kept only slightly better records than *her* duke.

She'd found a few interesting items and set them aside. She didn't want to bring them to Pemberth's attention until she was certain they actually meant something.

Aha! This was what she was looking for. A previously opened letter from *Findlay and Nottingham Imports and*

Exports. She opened the journal and confirmed her suspicions.

And then she realized that another note had been stuffed inside along with the statement. One that had very recognizable handwriting scrawled across it.

Her father's. Dated 19 August 1826

Your Grace,

As per your promise, made on 1 Sept, Year of our Lord, 1825, and since payment of eight thousand pounds has not been forthcoming, I demand you follow through with said alternative promise of marriage to my eldest daughter, Lila Catherine Breton, making her Duchess of Pemberth before 31 December of this year. Failure to comply will result in damages taken by three particularly unpleasant gentlemen in my employ.

Please acknowledge receipt of this demand within one fortnight.

Salutations,

Quimbly

ANOTHER NOTE in what Lila now recognized as Keenan's handwriting.

Paid in full, 30 August.

But this made no sense at all!

She traced back events in her mind. Blakely had called off his betrothal to her in June of 1825 and shortly afterward, her father had moved their family under what had seemed to be havey-cavey circumstances up to Bryony Manor.

Apparently, her father had negotiated some sort of devil's bargain with Pemberth's brother last summer.

But if Keenan had paid the debt in full, then why had Pemberth been forced to marry her?

She frantically began searching through the accounting journal once again. She needed to figure this out. Something was not right.

What if her Pemberth had married her under false pretenses?

What had really happened to Keenan?

There must be more here! She began opening drawers and checking for any files she might have missed. At the bottom of the lowest left-hand drawer, she noticed something odd. The drawer appeared shallow in depth.

Feeling like something of a sleuth, investigator, or *spy*, she located the knife she normally used to open envelopes and began wedging it around the wooden bottom.

Pop!

It lifted off. And beneath the false drawer, a small stack of papers sat innocently beckoning her to peruse.

Certificate of Death

She skimmed over the information.

Keenan David Timothy Saint-Pierre, Died 8 September, Year of our Lord 1826.

And then her eyes moved to the next line.

Cause of death: Suicide

"Has the desk finally consumed you completely?" Pemberth's voice had her slamming the drawer shut and jolting up. He obviously had not intended her to discover the death certificate. He would have informed her of the hidden papers if he'd wanted her to know.

Wouldn't he?

Something cold took hold of her heart at the information she'd discovered earlier. Why had he married her if the debt had been paid?

What has Father done now?

"Oh, um. Not yet." And then she forced a smile. "You're back early." Should she ask him now? He looked more handsome than ever today, dressed somewhat formally in a waistcoat and black jacket. He'd been visiting their neighbor on the north, an elderly man who wanted to thin his herds. Vincent had hoped he might be able to strike a bargain.

He did not keep a valet and so she'd tied his cravat earlier that morning. She blinked at the illogical notion that each day he did, indeed, appear even more handsome to her than he had the day before.

More lovable.

"Lord Oakley is willing to sell me the sheep on credit." He appeared quite satisfied with himself. She'd requested a subscription to *The Observer* and the first of the papers had arrived two days ago. He'd been quite right in that there was more profit in sheep than potatoes. "Come here and perhaps we can celebrate." His smile hinted at his lusty intent.

And without fail, her body was his to command.

A few suggestive words from him and her thighs turned to what felt like liquid jelly and her breasts ached with a need she'd never realized she had.

Debt paid in full.

For the first time, she wondered if she might be an imposter—his wife under false pretenses.

And yet her legs carried her to where he stood, and she daringly reached out to cover his manhood. The hardness she discovered there, almost without fail, had her tilting her head back for his kiss. "Did you lock the door?" she mumbled against his lips.

"Always," he answered back.

He walked her backward to the long settee where they'd already created a myriad of wicked memories and went to push her down to sit.

"No." She spun them around instead and pressed upon his shoulders.

He did not resist, and in the next instant sat sprawled in the middle of the settee, legs spread as he watched her with patient curiosity.

Lila had heard of such an act, and after he'd pleasured her so many times with his own mouth, wanted to see if she could achieve similar results.

She also wanted to know *it* more intimately— that piece of him that connected them together and had seemingly touched the deepest part of her.

She dropped her gaze to the fasteners on his breeches and at the same time, lowered herself to her knees. Before she could even reach for the buttons, his hands were already assisting her with the task.

"You don't have to." Married barely just over a fortnight and it seemed he could already read her mind.

"I know."

He tugged at his shirt and lowered the flap of his falls.

She'd caught glimpses of it before. She'd even held it in her hand a time or two. But this…

With silken skin, it was almost hot to the touch. He groaned when she placed her hand at the base, her fingers not quite capable of wrapping all the way around it.

It jumped. Almost of its own accord.

It was the most fascinating thing she'd ever laid eyes upon.

She leaned forward and—

"Your Grace!" There was a loud knocking on the door. "Are you in there? You have visitors!"

At this, Pemberth groaned, drawing a laugh from Lila. This was the first time since her arrival that anyone other than the steward or one of the local tradesmen had deigned to come visiting. Impeccable timing!

With a grimace, she rose and smoothed her skirts.

"One moment!" She moved slowly to the door in order to allow Pemberth a chance to... rearrange himself. It wouldn't do for his breeches to be standing at attention to receive their guest. Lila stifled a grin at the image. Poor man.

After a glance over her shoulder to ascertain he was presentable, Lila opened the door with what she hoped appeared to be a cool smile.

"Thought you were alone, Your Grace." Mrs. Smith peeked around her with a sly smile. "I've put Mr. and Mrs. Kemp as well as Miss Kemp in the front drawing-room. They're expecting you shortly."

Lila wished she'd been able to do something to improve the room, but it had not been high on her list of priorities.

Besides, she'd far preferred the coziness of Pemberth's study. She reached a hand out for her husband, who approached from across the room.

"In that case, we mustn't keep them waiting, must we? Pemberth?"

Three minutes later, Lila and Pemberth sat across from two of the nearby village's most elite citizens—and their daughter.

"Well, we never thought to send invitations up here before, it's been so long since Glenn Abby has had a duchess in residence. But I told Mr. Kemp I'd wager that a dignified young woman such as yourself, Your Grace, might be finding herself in need of some socializing." Mrs. Kemp was apparently in charge of the local charity and was heading up an assembly dance in two days' time. "I know it's late notice, but we aren't overly formal all the way up here, now are we, Lavinia?"

The younger woman had not even the decency to drag her gaze away from Pemberth when she nodded. Lila would have liked to reach across the small space between them. Drool needed wiping off of Miss Lavinia Kemp's chin.

Pemberth seemed oblivious to the young woman's attention.

But a dance! And other ladies and gentlemen with which to converse. It wasn't that Lila did not appreciate her husband's rather stimulating company, but it had been months since she'd been afforded such an opportunity.

"Would you care to attend?" Pemberth turned to her. "I know—"

"I'd love to!" She turned back to Mrs. Kemp. "And thank you so much for making the drive to invite us. Would you care for some tea?"

AN EVENING OUT

"Oh, my lady," Fran gushed. "I've never seen you looking so beautiful."

Lila studied her reflection in the mirror of her very own chamber.

Although the manor wasn't exactly teeming with servants, Lila and Fran had managed to oversee a thorough cleaning and refurbishing of the master's chambers and finally, Fran had been able to unpack all of her trunks.

She'd moved Pemberth into his larger chamber, and that night they'd share it together for the first time.

After the dance.

Feeling far too pleased with life than a lady ought, Lila twirled around in a circle, causing the gown to swirl around her.

She'd worn the gown before, and Fran had done her hair up with equal flair in the past. But she had to agree with her maid... she had a different look to her then before she'd married.

In the short time she'd spent with Pemberth, she'd changed.

If only Arianna could be here with here as well.

Lila had made casual mention a few times to Pemberth that she wished her sister could come and visit her, but it seemed he thought she meant next summer, or even later.

Meanwhile, Lila had no idea what new hell her father might be putting her sister through—without Lila to take the bulk of his criticism.

She jumped when a knock sounded on the adjoining door, suddenly feeling more than a little guilty for... being happy?

How could she be happy until her sister was safe?

"Come in," she beckoned.

Seeing her husband peer in made her feel better, and yet added to her guilt.

"I hadn't realized you were so far along with this project." He seemed hesitant to enter so she crossed the room to take his hand. He wore a black jacket and a ruby waistcoat embroidered with gold thread. His cravat hung untied around his neck and so Lila reached up to perform the task for him. She'd take any excuse to touch this man.

Fran disappeared into the dressing room.

"Of course, some of the furnishings are a little shabby, but they look rather lovely since we've had them painted." She looped off the knot and then gestured toward a cozy loveseat. "This was reupholstered."

With a somewhat curious but dazed expression, he released her hand to explore her chamber slowly, on his own.

"This is your sister?" He'd stopped before a small miniature she had standing on her bureau.

"Arianna." She nodded, that guilt returning to settle quite comfortably around her heart again. "I miss her."

He nodded and then moved along to the large box where she'd always kept her jewelry.

"May I?" he asked before opening it.

"Of course." She had nothing of real value. Her father had raided it before Fran could pack it up. Otherwise, she'd have told Pemberth to sell them in order to purchase the stocks he needed. "They're all fakes."

He opened the box and lifted a necklace and then a pendant. She found it oddly sweet that he thought her personal items interesting. Almost as though he might be coming to care—

"Lila? What is this?" She peered around him. He was holding the vial her mother had given her just before their wedding. So much had changed since then that she'd forgotten all about the strange gesture.

"A sleeping draught. My mother gave it to me." Although they had grown closer over the past few weeks, she dared not reveal to him that the potion had been given with him in mind.

His gaze flickered to her bed. "Do you find yourself missing your sleep? Have I kept you awake too often?"

"No!" That was the last thing in the world that she wanted. "I mean, no, you have not kept me up too often. I like sleeping with you. That is, I am not missing my sleep." By this time, she realized she must be blushing to the roots of her hair.

He turned to face her, feet shoulders' distance apart. "Good." Intensity flared from those silver-blue eyes of his. "We can use this bed, or we can use the one through the doorway. We will not require both."

Lila felt a grin tugging at her lips. "On the same night," she added.

"Just so we understand one another." That intensity of his had turned to wicked intent.

"Only we haven't time now, if we're to arrive at the assembly in time. How long did you say it would take us to get to the village? I'm so excited! I told you when I last mingled with society of any sort, have I not?" And then she found herself babbling. She was nervous.

Pemberth tugged her up against him and bent so that his lips nearly touched hers. "Everyone is going to love you. Even if you weren't so easy to love, they would have to." And then his lips dropped the softest of kisses upon hers. "Remember, Lila. You are a duchess."

She tilted her head back to gaze up at him. "And you are a duke." And then, feeling warmth spread through her limbs, she added, "My duke."

VINCENT HAD NOT ATTENDED a village assembly since before he'd reached his majority, and he'd been pleasantly surprised to discover that he'd enjoyed himself. Not because of the lukewarm watered-down lemonade, nor the rock-like biscuits, nor the slightly out of tune music.

But because of the woman on his arm.

She'd been a vision and he hadn't been the only one to think thusly. Gentlemen and ladies alike, upon being presented to her, approached her warily—but only for an instant. She'd enquired sweetly about their families, their homes, and had them eating out of her hand in no time at all.

Much later that night, Lila burrowed deeper into his body as he cradled her from behind. They'd chosen to utilize his chamber, after all. But despite a rigorous bout of lovemaking, her muscles tensed beside him.

"You enjoyed yourself this evening?" he whispered in her ear.

She nodded. "I did, but I cannot help but feel guilty that I have spent a most delightful evening, making friends, enjoying new challenges, and my sister is yet trapped at my father's home."

She'd mentioned her concerns a few times before. "Surely, your father will find her a husband as well? And then she can be free of him?"

Instead of soothing her, his words did the opposite. She twisted around and he could see her frowning in the moonlight from the window. She was none too happy with his response.

"As he did for me? Did my father vet you at all? He'd have just as well that I marry your brother! He knew nothing of you, only that you were a duke and that marrying you would make his daughter into a duchess."

"Are you not happy with the result?" Vincent didn't like the sting he felt at her words.

"That has nothing to do with it! I got lucky! There is no guarantee my father won't marry my sister off to some depraved lord, or worse!"

"What can be worse than a depraved lord?" He chuckled. She really was becoming overly dramatic about all of this.

Scowling even deeper now, she pushed herself to a sitting position. "You do not know my father as I do! You haven't had to live with the rumors of what he's done. He's tried to kill people. I'm not certain he's never succeeded."

"Lila." He pushed himself up on one elbow. This discussion was getting out of hand all too quickly. "Lie down. I doubt your father has killed anyone."

She resisted him when he tried to drag her down beside him, instead drawing back even farther. "You met him. Tell me you are convinced he would not hurt my sister."

Vincent rubbed his chin, remembering the way the man had torn the shawl from her shoulders and ruthlessly removed the pins from her hair. Vincent had been more concerned with his own problems at the time and only wanted to be on the road back home. But now that he remembered, the esteemed Earl of Quimbly had had something of a depraved look in his eyes.

"I will see what I can do."

But she was not to be calmed down. She sat on the bed facing him, her arms hugging her knees to her chest. "Pemberth." She shifted her gaze away guiltily. "I'm not certain your brother's debt to my father was not paid. I found a notation made by him that he'd paid it off in full. This estate is not destitute, as you believe. Keenan made some excellent investments. You did not have to marry me. My father took advantage of your brother's death by forcing—"

"Quimbly showed me the signed contract." What was she saying? "Why have you not told me this before?" He'd trusted her with all of the estate books. He'd trusted she'd share anything of particular interest with him.

She easily could have done this earlier, before the Kemps arrived.

She turned pleading eyes toward him. "I wanted to verify the investment income before mentioning anything. We need to meet with your brother's London solicitors. There are accounts…"

"And you thought I couldn't handle the disappointment if you were wrong? You think so little of me? Is that why you are only telling me this now?"

She squeezed her eyes tight. "I did not want you to be angry with me for something my father did. The debt had already been paid, Pemberth! Don't you see? You may have married me under false pretenses."

Vincent let out a sigh. He wanted to be angry with her for keeping something of such import from him. He'd thought…

"I think my father had something to do with your brother's death."

"You don't know what you're talking about, Lila." The only person he could blame for his brother's death was buried six feet underground. Vincent got out of bed, pulling on his breeches. "Leave it be!"

"But my father was not home at the time of your brother's death. He was gone on business. Is it possible that he came here? Is it—"

"Leave it, Lila!" Vincent had not, nor would he ever, discuss the nature or circumstance of Keenan's death with anyone. And not because of his own reputation. His brother had been his hero. The fact that Keenan had taken his own life would stain his legacy forever. Vincent wanted no one to know, not even his wife. He pulled on a shirt and then shoved his feet into his boots.

"Where are you going? Please, Vincent. Talk to me." The sight of her on her knees, begging him, ought to have been enough to soothe the torment she'd caused. But all he could see in that moment was his brother's face, eyes staring at nothing, on that dreadful day. All he could think was that his brother had willingly abandoned him.

He turned away. How had this happened? One moment he was imagining a future with her, loving her, and the next, he was questioning everything. None of this made sense. He ran one hand through his hair.

"Were you only using me as well, Lila? To get away from him?" Of course, she had been! She'd admitted as much.

"At first--"

"Am I handy only until you get your sister away from him as well?" And then it dawned on him. "Is that why you have been so happy to please me in bed?"

She drew back, almost as though he had slapped her. And he felt guilty but quashed it immediately. He'd been duped for his own stupidity. And then she'd kept vital financial information from him. She'd not even hinted about it—about any of it—until he'd resisted bringing her sister to Glenn Abbey.

The damn crux of it was he would have brought the girl here quickly enough if Lila had only batted her lashes a few times at him. He'd been utterly besotted with her.

What kind of a fool was he?

If only he hadn't been so such an idiot. If only he would have read the documents rather than shove them into a drawer. He jammed his hand into his jacket.

"Please don't go." He could see by the moonlight sparkling from her eyes that tears were threatening to fall. "Can we discuss this? Please?"

"Get some sleep, Lila. Take some of that draught your mother gave you."

And then he strode out, feeling as much loss as abject fury. He'd been used by her father. His brother had told him nothing of any investments. And then his brother betrayed him in the worst possible way.

And now she had used him. Stinging burned his eyes. Less than an hour ago, she'd been lying beneath him, straining for him to fill her more deeply.

He stormed down the stairs, skipping every other one and when he found himself in the foyer entrance, he knew there was only one person to answer for any of this.

And he was a hard day's ride away, damnit.

Vincent scribbled out a note in the salver and made his way to the stables. He'd have to awaken Calvin and Drake. But he'd have his answer, by God.

Whether he liked it or not.

MIDNIGHT JOURNEY

With a clear sky and a full moon, Vincent and two of his most dependable employees rode through the night, stopping only to change out their horses. By the time the sun rose to the center of the sky, he surmised he'd arrive at Bryony Manor within an hour.

He'd been rash to leave while in a temper. The thought plagued him now.

When she'd speculated that her father had something to do with Keenan's death, however, she'd stirred a suspicion he'd dared not contemplate before.

His brother was not the sort of man to kill himself over financial ruin. Their father had fought against seemingly insurmountable adversity to keep the dukedom strong, as had their grandfather before them. More than once, Keenan had shown the same strength of the men who'd preceded him as Duke of Pemberth.

Quimbly knew something and, by God, Vincent was going to find out what it was.

And after that…

Vincent would return to his wife, her sister in tow, so long as he wasn't required to kidnap the girl, and he'd make known to Lila his feelings regarding their marriage once and for all.

Because after sitting in the saddle for hours on end, he'd turned the circumstances over in his mind quite thoroughly.

She'd had reason to fear her father before their marriage, and he'd been an ass not to acknowledge this the night before. She merely feared for her sister. Of course, she'd seek protection for her as well!

To hell with the fact that she hadn't told him right away; they weren't in dun territory after all. She'd been going through papers for days now, and she'd only wanted to be certain before getting his hopes up.

He owed her one hell of an apology.

He loved her. It frustrated him that he hadn't said it before, that he only realized it when he could do nothing about it.

He shouldn't have left. At least not in anger.

A dark cloud drifted over the sun, sending a chill through him at the same time Bryony Manor appeared in the distance.

She'd said she thought her father could have had something to do with Keenan's death. Was it possible Quimbly had been at Glenn Abby?

Vincent rolled his shoulders. He would not have known. He'd spent most of his time in the fields. He should have been paying attention. The thought that he'd inherit the title had never entered his mind. Ever.

Only after turning onto the short road leading to the front manor steps, did he become aware of a flurry of frantic activity. One of the manservants had mounted a horse and was riding toward them.

"Ho, there!" Vincent held up a hand. He vaguely remembered this particular servant from his prior visit. On that occasion, the man, who'd been ever-present in Quimbly's shadow, had seemed inordinately loyal to his employer.

The servant pulled hard on his horse, having recognized Vincent immediately. "He won't take her back so you're wasting your time. I'm to fetch the physician. The master is ill!" As quick as that, the man spurred his horse and raced off the property.

Vincent met Calvin's gaze and then the two of them urged their horses toward the manor, arriving at the entrance in a matter of seconds. A young girl had stepped outside and for a moment, Vincent had to blink his eyes, almost certain she was his wife.

"Lady Arianna?"

The girl nodded, eyeing him suspiciously.

Vincent landed on the ground and handed off his mount. "I am Pemberth."

"Where is my sister?" She lifted her chin in a remarkably familiar gesture.

"She has sent for you." But if Quimbly was ill, Vincent might be running out of time. "Take me to your father." He would have some answers while he was here.

Lila's sister studied him for a moment, as though measuring his character.

"And then have your maid pack your things. My wife desires her sister's company at her new home."

At these words, she finally sprang into action. "This way." She led him up the stairs and around but one corner.

As they neared the master suites, the sounds of weeping drifted out from one of the chambers.

Lady Arianna stopped at the door. "Agnes, leave them be a moment."

An older servant, eyes red and swollen, peeked out of the chamber with an anxious gaze. "Is he the physician?"

"I—" Vincent began.

"He is. Step away please." Lady Arianna was obviously made of the same stock as his wife. He'd have found humor in the two sisters' stubbornness under other circumstances.

Once the woman had reluctantly backed out, Vincent followed the girl into her father's chamber.

Not one, but two people laid on the bed.

On the nearest side, a man, Quimbly, his skin a parchment-like white, his lips blue, his eyes...

Gazing lifelessly at the ceiling.

An uncovered chamber pot sat on the table beside him emitting a vomitus odor: a foul, almost chemical stench that stirred a vague memory in the back of Vincent's mind.

"Mama?" Lady Arianna had gone to the other side of the bed and leaned over her mother.

"I took care of him, darling." The countess' words barely sounded between her gasping breaths. And then the woman held out her hand atop the coverlet and slowly opened her fingers. Inside of her hand lay two vials. Lady Quimbly chuckled. "Gave him a taste of his own, my dearest Arianna."

Seeing it in her hand, smelling the stench of death, Vincent was not mistaken. It was the same vial he'd found in his brother's palm. The same red cap. The same traces of powdery substance lining the glass.

"No more," the countess said, sounding weaker. "He's taken too many lives, hurt too many people."

Lila's sister's shoulders began to shake, the magnitude of this moment in time penetrating her calm. "But why you, Mama?" She pressed her cheek beside her mother's.

"He killed my brother?" It wasn't really a question. But Vincent needed to know.

The woman finally seemed to notice he was in the room. Meeting his eyes, she nodded. "My husband needed a duchess for a daughter. I never understood. But your brother refused to marry her. My poor Lila. She'd already been rejected once."

Vincent struggled between the relief he felt to learn his brother hadn't taken his own life and anger at the dead man lying on the bed.

Disgusted by all the tragedies caused by a madman, Vincent accepted the former emotion and dismissed the latter.

It was over.

The sudden desire to leave all of this behind and return to Lila was all that mattered now. She was his life now. Lila...

"YOU LOVE MY OLDEST DAUGHTER?" the countess implored him. "She is happy?" Her breathing had become labored. If she'd swallowed the arsenic, she was likely moments from death, nothing could be done.

"I love her." Vincent's own throat felt thick. "She is happy." And she would be, too, as soon as he could get home and clear up all of their misunderstandings.

The countess fell back with closed eyes. "She won't be needing my sleeping draught then."

~

VINCENT RODE as though the hounds of hell chased him. Thank God for the moonlight. Thank God a horse had been available at the last inn, a good, strong horse.

He never would have driven an animal so hard, but...

His wife.

He dared not contemplate what he might find at his own home.

Please, don't go! She'd begged him.

And his words. Words he'd regret for the rest of his life. Words said out of temper, and hurt, and shame: *Get some sleep, Lila. Take some of that draught your mother gave to you.*

Why hadn't he recognized it then? The vial was the same as the one he'd discovered with Keenan. He'd been so blinded by his own damn pride. He allowed the horse to slow to a walk. He could not make any animal run such a great distance. He'd be more the villain for doing so.

And then he realized... he could run.

He was close. He could not sit atop a horse ambling along while...

He could run. The horse would follow.

Vincent dismounted, landed on the ground, and settled into a pace he could maintain for a great distance, pumping his arms and legs, punishing himself in the only way he knew how. Ironically enough, the horse chose to trot beside him.

Vincent ran faster.

If she'd done as he told her, he'd never forgive himself.

Let her have been stubborn. Let her have defied her stupid ass husband. His mind alternated between chastising chants and desperate prayers.

FOURTEEN HOURS EARLIER

*H*e'd left her. She'd been right to fear his reaction upon learning the truth. Staring at her from the shadows, hurt had filled his eyes. And then came the anger. It had rolled off him in waves as he'd donned the clothes he'd worn earlier that evening. He'd been unable to remain even for the night in the same house with his wife.

She had wanted to please him so that he would help her save Arianna. *At first.* That had been her reason *at first.*

But could she have acted the same with anyone else?

She could not have!

Only him.

After the door slammed shut behind him, she'd sat frozen on the bed, waiting for him to return. Hoping he'd only gone for a ride to cool his temper.

She'd learned many of his habits during the weeks since they'd married. Being out of doors, with his horse or tending to one of the herds—it cleared his head—helped him think.

And so she'd waited.

The next morning, she'd discovered the note in the salver and that was when terror had set in.

He'd gone to confront her father. Her father was not a man who took well to any person to question his actions.

Pemberth was a large man, a strong man. But he was also an honorable one.

Her father would use that against him.

She'd wished to depart for Bryony Manor right away but Pemberth's driver had fled with him. Knowing Vincent was not to be alone while confronting her father gave her some small comfort. Calvin would be at his side, as well.

Two sturdy and loyal men.

All morning, she paced the stone corridors, fighting the urge to go after him. At the end of one particularly long hallway, she found herself staring at a painting. He'd pointed it out to her that first week.

Keenan. The former duke. His brother. Lila had come to know the man's handwriting almost better than her own, she'd gone over so many documents, read pages and pages of his correspondence.

Vincent's brother had been a good man whom her husband must have loved as much as Lila did Arianna.

How must he have hurt to believe Keenan had taken his own life? And yet…

It did not make sense.

Feeling a sense of purpose for the first time all day, she strode back to the library, opened the bottom drawer, and withdrew the secret documents once again. Letters between the local magistrate and Pemberth.

Arsenic poisoning. Small glass vial discovered in the

deceased's hand. And then she discovered the most damning evidence of all.

The suicide note.

My dearest brother,

The coffers are empty. We're in too much debt to save the dukedom. I cannot continue this way. Please contact the Earl of Quimbly who can be found at Bryony Manor to finalize payment of my debts.

Signed,

Keenan

If she hadn't read through the falsehood of the note, she would most certainly have known who'd written it by the extra twirl on the tail of the "Q" in her father's name.

The note had been forged.

Her father was despicable. He'd killed Keenan. Likely he'd not been alone, he would have taken Egan and Stan, his two most loyal brutes along to assist him.

Pemberth did not have to live out his life thinking his brother had committed the unforgivable sin.

Come back to me, love. Come home!

The remainder of the afternoon she spent matching investments with notices sent of incoming shipments. Her brother-in-law had not impoverished his estate, quite the contrary.

Lila would show Pemberth everything if—no—*when* he returned. Because, of course, he would return to her!

Only not on this day.

After what felt like hours of tossing and turning, unable to sleep, Lila slid off of the tall bed in her husband's chamber where she'd slept since his departure. She could take the draught. Get some rest tonight. If he did not return by tomorrow, she would enlist one of the other male servants to ride with her to Bryony Manor. Her father had killed at least once, that she knew of. He'd not hesitate to kill again.

Lila slipped through the adjoining door into her own chamber and once inside, slid open the drawer of her jewelry box and withdrew the velvet bag.

Holding up the vial of white powder, she realized she'd probably need some water.

Should she take all of it? Her mother hadn't specified. Had she?

Use it on your husband, her mother had advised. Likely this meant that Lila would only require half the amount to sleep.

She lifted a nearby pitcher and poured some tepid water into a matching glass and then emptied a little less than half the contents of the vial.

She would sleep tonight. Tomorrow could turn out to be a very long day, indeed. He had to be all right! *Please let him be unharmed. Please?*

She closed her eyes, lifted the glass to her lips, and—

Something solid and wet and cold sent the glass flying from her hand.

Pemberth! Shock replaced her worry in an instant.

She hadn't even heard him enter.

Without saying a single word, he tugged her tightly to him.

He was here! She wound her arms around his waist, feeling only relief as she pressed herself against her husband. He dripped with sweat despite the cold of the night air, but she did not care. His heart pounded rapidly beneath her ear. She didn't mind that her nightgown absorbed the damp from his clothing. She slid her hands up to his neck and tilted her head back, taking in his haggard appearance.

"You didn't drink it? The sleeping draught?"

She shook her head. "I never meant to hide anything—"

"It was poison! I thought I'd lost you." He swallowed hard, searching her eyes, his hands running over her arms, her shoulders...

Poison? She shook her head. "It was for sleep." She had just been going to drink it. "You knocked it from my hand. I haven't slept since you left..."

He shuddered, looking pained. "Thank God. It was poison and I told you to take it and then I saw the same vial... I had to get here."

What was he saying? Her mother had given it to her to subdue her husband. Had she actually told her it was for sleep? Or had Lila simply assumed...? "Poison?"

He nodded, and then swept her up against him again.

Her mother had told her to use it on *her husband!* Lila could have killed him! Confused and horrified, she clutched him back, just as tightly.

I could have killed him!

Ice cold clutched at her heart.

Oh, Mother, why?

But she knew. She'd suspected what her own mother had endured for years.

Dear God, she'd nearly taken it herself.

Pemberth tilted her head back and claimed her mouth with an onslaught so desperate that it was almost painful.

The good kind of painful.

A life affirming kind of painful.

Her heart overflowed with emotion at the same time her

body hungered for her husband. "I'm sorry," she managed to gasp against his lips.

"No. Oh, God, Lila. I am the one who is sorry." He lifted her and she wound her legs around his waist. A need unlike any she'd known consumed her. The need to become one with this man again. A need to show her love in every way. She needed...

Him.

Dragging his mouth along her neck, her shoulders, he walked them both forward and backed her up against the wall. "My love. I thought I'd lost you."

My love.

One of his hands released her to unfasten and then tug at his breaches. She didn't wait.

She did not need him to prepare her. Taking hold of his length, Lila placed him at her opening.

He pressed inside. No hesitation. No questions or play.

He knew what she wanted. She ached to be filled.

This was what she'd been made for—to join with this man.

This man. "Vincent." His name escaped on a rasping breath.

He was her other half. Together, two imperfect souls made perfect. They would seal their forgiveness and their trust and their love in an act as old as time. They would renew the promises they'd already sewn between one another.

Lila arched her back, grasping his arms with her hands at the same time his teeth tore at her gown, exposing all of her for him to consume. Like a storm that had hovered on the horizon, passion overtook them both. Lila moved with him. Deeper. Harder. Her heart sang as they mated together in their own unique rhythm, Obliterating any uncertainty. Their physical bodies said what words could never comprehend.

Gasps and moans melded with the sounds of flesh against flesh as he satisfied them both.

The wall shook behind her. Her legs trembled but it was he who held her up, he who pumped forcefully, increasing in both intensity and pace.

"Vincent!" He was her protector, her giver of pleasure.

Two last thrusts, each seemingly touching the core of her body and then, pinning her between his own body and the wall, he spent inside of her.

They stood that way, taking deep breaths, in a silence that quickly began filling with questions.

Lila grasped him around the neck once again and leaned forward.

In a rasping breath, she barely managed to whisper two words. "What happened?"

BITTERSWEET

What happened?

Vincent lowered her feet to the ground, sliding out of her while he did so, but kept one arm wrapped around her as he fastened his breeches.

At that moment, he never wanted to let her out of his sight again.

"Why would my mother give me poison?" She stepped back, causing his arm to drop away.

He had wanted this season to be a happy one for her. It was likely she hated her father, but she'd had hope for her mother. Staring at the broken glass spread at the other end of the room, he scrubbed one hand down his face.

"Your mother..." He couldn't just blurt it out. Not in here. Not with the sweet sickly smell of arsenic hovering in the air.

Not giving her a chance to resist, he scooped her up and carried her into the master's chamber.

His chamber.

Their chamber.

Her concerned look revealed that she sensed his news was not going to be good. He did not want to tell her this. After lowering her to the bed, he climbed up and gathered her against him, wanting more than anything to protect her from the truth he must impart, holding her head against his heart.

"Your mother..." He swallowed hard. "She has passed." And because she would find out anyway, he would not hide her parents' manner of death. "She poisoned both your father and herself. I saw the vial in her hand. It was then I realized..."

A gust of wind shook the window, but aside from the rattling of the windowpane, the room fell silent. Her head tucked into his chest, she did not speak or move. She simply absorbed the horror of his news.

"Arianne?" He was relieved to hear her voice, shaking though it was.

"Was with your mother in the end. She's strong, like you. Calvin and Drake are bringing her and the governess behind me. I would have stayed with her myself but when I saw what they'd taken, and I realized it was the same vial you'd shown me..." He could not explain the terror he'd felt at the thought that he'd lost her.

And then he closed his eyes. "Lila, it was the same vial Keenen clutched in his hand in death."

This information did not seem to surprise her. "My father forged the suicide note," she murmured against him. Of course, she had discovered the certificate. The damned secret drawer.

"I didn't want to believe he could take his own life." But he was speaking of his own brother and this was not about him. "Love, your mother said she needed to stop him."

She nodded beneath his chin. "She hated him, but she also loved him." And then a sob tore through her. "We all did. It doesn't make sense." And then another sob. "I hated him, Pemberth. I hated him."

Vincent wished he could take her pain. "I know, love. I know." He stroked her hair. How had this slip of a woman come to mean so much to him?

"She gave me the draught for you." At first, he wasn't certain he heard right. "She told me to give it to you, that it would put you to sleep if you were too demanding of me." She began trembling. "I hate them both, Pemberth. I hate them! I hate them."

He felt helpless. All he could do was absorb her cries, her tears, while the storm within her subsided.

She'd fall silent, seemingly asleep, but then a tremor would run through her and she'd weep gently once again. Not until the sun crept over the horizon did exhaustion and worry finally have its way with both of them. Holding tightly to one another, they slept.

HER FIRST THOUGHT, even before opening her eyes, was that her head hurt. The next was that she was not alone.

He came back.

And then the events that occurred at Bryony Manor roared into her memory. Could it all have been a nightmare? But no. It had not been.

Her mother had killed her father and then herself. Her mama. *Oh, Mama!*

Warm lips settled on her forehead. "You are awake?"

Her eyes ached as she opened them. They would be puffy and swollen. She could feel the grit from her leftover tears. And yet, she tilted her head back to look up at him. "I am. How did you know?"

Achingly familiar eyes studied her in concern. Shadows had etched themselves beneath them and stubble the color of a lion's mane darkened the lower half of his face. "I could feel your breathing change." He gave her a weak attempt at a smile.

"You came back to me."

Again, that weak smile. How had his become such a precious face? "I am back. I never should have left." Gentle fingertips grazed her cheek. "Will you forgive me?"

Lila blinked. "Will you forgive me?"

And then he dropped a kiss on her lips. No demand. No need. Just a kiss of affection and acceptance. "Nothing to forgive."

"Vincent." She tested his name on her lips. "I have nothing to forgive of you, either."

His smile spread wider this time. How could they smile after all that had come to pass? She could smile because she lov—

"I love you, Lila." His smile settled into simple contentment. "Your father was an evil, horrid man, but I will always have him to thank for forcing me into your life. And now that you are here, I'll do everything I know to keep you happy. You are a blessing to me. I would marry you a thousand times over if I could. Never doubt my love." His gaze revealed a hint of hidden savagery. "Never."

Lila swallowed hard. He was right. Without the damnable man she had called father, she would never have found this.

Him.

Love.

This absolute *knowing* that she was exactly where she was meant to be.

She had discovered her destiny, the man of her body and heart. "I love you, Vincent." She wound her arms around his neck. They would climb out of this bed today, bathe, eat, and make their plans for the future.

They would bring Arianna here, and they would mourn together and allow the scars of their childhood begin to heal.

They had survived and they had one another. Lila would shower her sister with all the love she deserved. Because despite everything, they had survived.

And life meant nothing without love.

Lila's heart swelled. She had been given more than her fair share.

Vincent climbed out of their tall bed, walked over to the window, and drew back the curtain.

Sometime in the night, her husband had removed his clothing. Lila licked her lips as she studied the sinewy ridges that made up his beautiful physique.

She'd been given hope and life and love and oh, so much more.

Her eyes trailed up the length of his legs and stopped just below his hips. She licked her lips again.

So very much more.

EPILOGUE

UNLIKELY FRIENDS

*L*ila frowned as she watched Adrianna spin around on the dance floor at her very first ton ball. The gentleman who'd claimed this particular dance seemed far too old for Lila's little sister. Not quite eight and ten, Adrianna had finally convinced Lila and Vincent that she was more than ready to make her come out to society this spring.

Lila bit her lip. Her little sister looked so very grown up and very, very pretty. Perhaps too pretty.

The music echoed across the gleaming parquet floors and chandeliers sparkled from above. After having been away from London for so long, it was all a little over-whelming.

"She will be fine," Vincent whispered in her ear. "She has her sister's beauty but also her wits." He squeezed her hand. "And if any one of the blokes sniffing around her makes so much as a single misstep, she will have the benefit of her brother-in-law's fist plowing through their face." Lila couldn't help but smile upon hearing that overly protective growl in her husband's voice.

He made for an excellent, if not somewhat overbearing, older brother to Adrianna.

"I know and I'm so very proud of her," Lila responded as she watched the couples execute the dance.

Vincent's breath caressed her cheek as he leaned in closer. "Would anyone notice, do you think, if we were to disappear for ten or twenty minutes? As lovely as you look tonight, the sight of you in that gown is making me rather uncomfortable and I'm not certain I have the patience to—
"

"Pardon me, Your Graces?" An oddly familiar voice cut off the inappropriate suggestion Vincent was about to make.

Marcus Roberts, Lila's former betrothed, stood before them with the woman she presumed to be his wife at his side.

"Your Grace." Lila nodded, unsure of what he might want to say to her. She was not angry with him. She'd never loved him. But her father had espoused him to be the most despicable of gentlemen after he'd broken their betrothal contract.

The Duke of Waters turned toward the petite brown-haired lady standing at his side. "Emily, I'd like to present you to the Duke and Duchess of Pemberth, Your Graces, this is my wife, the Duchess of Waters."

Lily flicked a glance toward Vincent. She'd explained her previous betrothal to her husband months and months ago, shortly after they married and from the wariness in his eyes, he had remembered the man's identity.

She smiled at him reassuringly and then, curious as to

what this was all about, Lila curtseyed to the other duchess who curtseyed back with a smile.

In all honesty, Lila could not remember if duchesses were supposed to curtsey to one another. After being married for a year and a half and keeping to their country estate for the most part, she hadn't as yet met any other duchesses.

She could not help herself, however, but take the measure of the other woman.

Upon being jilted by Marcus Roberts, Lila had been told by her father that her betrothed had married a Miss Emily Goodnight. The horrid woman was, he had insisted, an antidote, a vile and most disagreeable spinster who would long be remembered as the ugliest of all the duchesses in England.

Yet another thing he'd lied about.

Although Miss Goodnight, Her Grace, wore spectacles perched upon her nose, slightly askew no less, she was really, rather pretty.

And by the look in the duke of Water's eyes, Marcus Roberts was obviously enamored with her.

"My sympathy on your father's passing." Lila murmured, remembering that the duke's father had passed shortly after her father moved them up to Bryony Manor.

Waters cocked one brow. "My sympathies to you, as well, Your Grace." He turned to Vincent. "Perhaps, Pemberth, you'll take a smoke with me on the terrace, while the ladies, ah, get to know one another?"

Vincent met Lila's gaze and she nodded. He would know that this meeting might be uncomfortable.

"I would like for nothing more than to become acquainted with Her Grace." She consented.

Both ladies watched the backs of the gentlemen as they strolled toward the terrace doors. Lila surmised that although the young Duke of Waters cut a fine figure of a man, he paled in comparison to her husband. Vincent had a far superior––

"I have wanted to apologize to you for a very long time, and when I heard that you and Pemberth had come to London, I absolutely insisted Marcus introduce the two of us." The other lady touched Lila's arm lightly and drew them toward the wall.

Did Lila want an apology? She studied the other woman who seemed quite friendly and open and was not at all the witch her father had made her out to be.

"But I am quite content with the outcome, Your Grace. You have no need to apologize." Lila had considered this before. In fact, perhaps she ought to thank the other woman.

The Duchess nodded as though in agreement.

"Emily," She said. "Please call me Emily. Far too much Your Gracing all around if I do say so myself." She scrunched her nose, making her seem even more approachable and friendly. "The thing of it is, I intentionally set out to convince your betrothed to jilt you. I am not sorry for that as I would not give him up for all the gold in the kingdom, but I am sorry that you were hurt as a result of my actions. And I am most sorry that you were forced to remain in your father's custody, villain that he was."

Lila had not thought anyone would speak so bluntly of her father in London, let alone at a ball.

"Few people crossed my father and emerged unscathed." Lila could not help but wonder what all had occurred when he'd discovered the couple's temerity. "But, you are... happy?"

"We are." The other woman's gaze shifted in the direction of the terrace. "And you, Your Grace?"

Lila could not help but grin. "I am." And then she added. "All is well that ends well. And please call me Lila."

Lila hadn't been allowed to become close to other women for most of her life. Since her marriage, although she'd become acquainted with a few of their neighbors, the ladies maintained a certain aloofness. Lila's station was something of a barrier.

How wonderful it would be to have an actual friend. "I had forgotten the splendor of a *ton* ball." She put forth.

Again, the duchess, *Emily*, scrunched up her nose, making her glasses jump up and then settle again, this time quite evenly. She leaned closer to Lila. "You'll have the most fun in the library, let me assure you." Emily smiled quite unapologetically.

"What would one want to do in a library when there is a ball...?"

The other lady winked, and Lila couldn't help but burst into laughter. It was no wonder Emily Goodnight had so easily caught herself a husband.

"In addition to that, if we were to stroll through the gardens, we'd overhear all manner of interesting goings-on."

Lila laughed again. "Who needs to dance with so many other offerings for entertainment?"

"My sentiments exactly." Emily smiled and then, suddenly distracted, waved at someone beyond Lila's shoulder. "I must warn you, we are about to be bombarded on all sides. Some of my dearest friends are approaching––you will absolutely love them."

Excited cries of "Emily!" And then,"Cecily! Sophia! Rhoda!" had Lila taking a step back. Three other ladies, all lovely and obviously old friends––very good friends–– hugged and fawned over one another, asking about babies and husbands and travels making Lila feel more than a little like an interloper.

Before she could make her excuses, Emily grasped hold of Lila's wrist and introduced her to all of them. They all seemed to know exactly who Lila was, but welcomed her enthusiastically, asking her about her marriage and her journey to London and even invited her along on an excursion to Bond Street with all of them the next day.

"We're going to visit Madam Chantal and will insist that she fit you into our appointments. I have the most inspiring idea for a dress for you." The red haired lady suggested in a friendly manner that Lila was most unaccustomed to.

"Puffed sleeves past the elbows?" One of them asked.

"Yes, and a low back, what with such a lovely complexion."

Lila could hardly keep up with them. It was overwhelming and frightening and... absolutely one of the most delightful things to have happened to her since they'd arrived in town.

Was it possible that she might make some friends in London? Despite all the sins of her father?

"I have a sister here," Lila's gaze searched for Adrianna and then located her, sitting along the wall and chatting, most animatedly, with two other girls seated beside her.

"Oh, she has met Hollyhock and Coleus, my younger sisters." The tallest of the girls, but also the most... sensual looking of them, commented.

"And that is Althea, one of Devlin's younger cousins."

The tiny blond woman, who, ironically enough, was yet another duchess, chimed in,

"They are sitting in the exact spot the four of us met." Cecily, the redhead smiled at all of them. "Do you remember?"

Rhoda cocked her head. "Were we not closer to the windows?"

"No, that is the exact spot." Emily confirmed quite adamantly.

"But should they remain sitting? Should they not be mingling so that they might all be asked to dance?" Lila wondered aloud.

"Absolutely not!" Emily Goodnight put one arm slightly around Lila's shoulders. "Because being a wallflower is one of the most important aspects of having a London Season."

Lila raised her brows in question.

"Finding oneself a husband is absolutely divine," Sophia explained in a hushed whisper. "But a girl must have good friends who will always have her back." She locked arms with Lila.

"And tell her if her hem has come undone, or if gentlemen are betting on her." Rhoda added.

Cecily grinned. "Or if she has had too much champagne."

Lila couldn't help but think how lovely all of that would be.

She sighed and glanced back to where the younger girls sat chatting.

"I did not realize this." She admitted shyly.

"Well, now you do." Emily lowered her spectacles and winked. "Sometimes… we go so far as to discuss the attributes of various mentulas…

All of them burst out laughing and Sophia blushed to the

roots of her hair. "Enough Emily! You're going to scare our new friend away!"

Lila just barely caught sight of Vincent, standing with the Duke of Waters and three other very impressive looking gentlemen. All of them glanced over at them upon hearing the laughter.

Vincent appeared content and smiled at Lila warmly.

Perhaps later she would slip away with him to the library, but for now she wished to learn more about her new friends.

She turned back to the ladies. "What exactly is a *mentula*...?"

***

Thank you so much for reading Lila and Vincent's quest for a happily ever after! This Novella concludes the Devilish Debutantes series. To begin another amazing series by Annabelle we suggest **The Perfect Debutante** which is book 1 of the Perfect Regency series by Annabelle.

HEIR TO A DUKE, A DEBUTANTE AND AN ARRANGED MARRIAGE It couldn't have been any more perfect... Miss Louella Rose is Sweet, Beautiful. Refined. The answer to all her family's woes. But beneath her flawless complexion, behind her mesmerizing eyes, she hides a secret shame. STANTON promised to marry the woman of his father's choice by the age of thirty and that time has finally come. To his surprise and delight, the chosen lady is the perfect debutante, for him anyhow, and he couldn't be happier... until he discovers the scars that make no sense – scars that shatter the illusion of perfection. LIES, greed and blood lay waste to a most promising marriage. Can their love overcome the ravages of guilt and carry them through life's imperfections?

The Perfect Debutante

Here is your free sneak peek!

CHAPTER 1- THE PERFECT DEBUTANTE

THE DARKNESS

*M*iss Louella Rose Redfield huddled on the floor on the far side of the large canopied bed taking up most of her chamber. If her mother took it upon herself to peek in, she would believe the room to be empty and leave.

Which was exactly what Louella wanted—what she needed.

It wasn't as though she were a child! She was a lady now. She had every right to be left alone. She glanced toward the closed door.

Mama would not come now anyhow. Mama and Papa knew she was not at all pleased with them. Not after Papa had told her his decision and given her no choice but to consent to the betrothal he'd arranged for her with their neighbor's son.

And they expected her to be grateful! Of all things!

Anger. Frustration. Disappointment. The hopelessness of this situation made her want to be invisible. Black crept into the edges of her vision.

How could her parents so easily dismiss her older sister Olivia? They couldn't realize the cruelty of their actions. For this slight seemed worse than all the others. To betroth the younger daughter first.

Her.

Cowering behind the bed, Louella opened the bottom drawer of the nightstand and reverently withdrew the sewing basket.

The tattered straw and old cloth lining provided a modicum of comfort, in and of itself.

Her father's words replayed in her head. "You are the beauty of this family, Louella. A perfect English Rose. This is your duty. And your mother assures me the marquess is quite handsome. You'll be a duchess someday, gel. Now stop your blathering." He'd meant to placate her.

A beauty! Perfect?

Louella knew what they saw.

A young girl with an unblemished complexion, shining chestnut hair, and eyes the color of the sky, framed with thick lashes.

But that was only her shell.

She was not perfect; she was not beautiful.

Dizziness gripped her.

Closing her eyes, Louella inhaled deeply before opening them again and unraveling the ribbon from around her wrist. She'd tied the silk loosely, but it managed to leave an imprint on the tender flesh, nonetheless.

She opened the basket and withdrew what she sought. Eyeing it critically, she frowned. The needle was becoming dull from too much use.

She could not access her abdomen during the daytime. Her stays prevented that.

Examining her arm, she located an unscarred section. With practiced precision, she compelled the needle downward. As the sharp point drew a short crimson line, she felt nothing.

She pressed harder the second time, and a thicker line of blood oozed onto her pale, almost translucent skin. A sting. And tingling. *Ah, yes. I'm real.*

And the berating voices swirling in her mind began to subside.

Blood is real.

The blood is mine.

I am real.

She drew another line, this one longer and just the tiniest bit deeper than the first two. The needle stung. It hurt even.

Her racing heart slowed.

It would be okay. Olivia would understand.

She could now feel the floor beneath her and the frame of the bed digging into her back.

The last cut was shallow, barely a scratch, really.

Her vision cleared.

As she watched blood flow and begin to congeal, her breathing slowed as her muscles relaxed. Sleep called to her, the sensation of melting into the floor overcoming all her senses. Still caressing the needle between her fingers, she dropped her hand to the carpet and tilted her head back, resting it on the side of the bed.

She could do this. She didn't want to, but she could. Papa would insist.

After what may have been a few seconds, or several moments, Louella roused herself from the blessed lethargy enough to clean the needle and replace it in the sewing basket.

She then washed her wrist in the wash basin, dried it, rewrapped the silk ribbon, and tied it snugly.

Using her teeth, she managed a fairly decent bow.

Louella had done this before.

The devil didn't dwell inside her.

It was just... her.

~

"You wish me to marry *little Louella Rose?*"

Captain Cameron Samuel Benjamin Denning, Marquess of Stanton, barely remembered the girl.

She'd been a child when he left, gallivanting about her father's estate and often his father's property as well.

He vaguely remembered the older sister... blonde, she'd been on the verge of womanhood, sweet and pretty. But he'd been an arrogant Devil at the time. All he'd noticed was that the gel had been cockeyed.

And the younger girl? Louella Rose? She had been all skin and bones, brilliant blue eyes too large for her face, dirt on her dresses, and ah, yes, stringy brown hair. She would have been most unmemorable but for her flashing eyes and violent temper. She'd lobbed an apple at his head on one occasion.

He scratched his chin. If memory served him correctly, he'd done something to provoke the attack. He'd been an ass that summer. Hating his father. Hating his father's new family. Hating pretty much everybody, including himself.

"She's not a child anymore," his father said without glancing up from the papers on his desk.

What had the sister's name been? Olive? No, Olivia, Miss Olivia Redfield, oldest daughter of the Viscount Hallewell. She'd been closer to him in age.

"Truth be told," his stepmother, the duchess, piped in, "Miss Louella Rose is one of the comeliest debutantes in all of England."

Cameron wasn't certain he could believe that. The hoyden had been something of a tomboy, trespassing with her sister almost daily. They'd met with better luck fishing on the ducal lands than their own.

And Cameron had not treated them kindly. Ah, yes, he'd teased the older girl mercilessly for her eye. He winced at the memory.

At the time, he'd barely reached his majority; he'd been an irresponsible youth, willing to do anything to escape his father and all of his ducal expectations.

"What of the older daughter?" Cameron stared out the window, contemplating his past wrongs.

Again, his stepmother supplied the answer. "Something of a spinster. Doesn't move in Society, as I understand. Hallewell keeps her well under wraps. I doubt they've brought her with them to London for the Season. If I were to take a guess, I'd say she's probably simple."

His father grunted.

Cameron knew neither of the girls were what attracted his father to such an alliance. The Hallewell estate sat just south of Ashton Acres. Nestled in the low lands, unkempt and overrun with brush, it was aptly named Thistle Park.

But just inside of its borders sat the true prize.

An abandoned mine.

Abandoned, and branded as cursed by the current viscount's father following a disastrous cave-in decades ago. But that wasn't the end of it. No, the damn thing was rumored to be loaded with gold. A few of the men who'd managed to survive the collapse, but not their injuries, had spoken of a thick vein discovered just before the tragedy. Ancient tales warned that the cave-in had occurred because the treasure had been exposed.

Locals scoffed at the notion of the mine having anything of value. Never, in the history of the area, the entire region, really, had any precious metals been mined profitably.

Viscount Hallewell, like his father before him, believed the mine to be cursed. He'd adamantly refused to reopen it. Until now, apparently.

With pockets to let, and a comely daughter at that... Cameron guessed that Crawford, his own father, had finally discovered the bargaining chip to change Hallewell's mind.

His son.

And, fiend seize it, upon departing a decade ago, Cameron had promised to marry upon his return. He'd not hated his birthright; he'd simply needed to sow his oats. Such a stupid promise to have made.

"Isn't there a boy in the family as well?" Surely, the son would have something to say about all of this. It was his inheritance, after all.

"Not anymore. Died shortly after your departure." Cameron's father had no sympathy when it came to others' misfortunes.

Raising his brows, Cam glanced toward the duchess. She would know more about the family.

"William, I believe they called him, couldn't have been older than six or seven at the time," she replied helpfully.

"His mother, the viscountess, was inconsolable for months. But the boy was always sickly. Nearly drowned but then took ill. I imagine he'd have died of some other malady if not for the accident."

Cam rubbed his eyes with the heels of his hands. All of this seemed rather sudden, and yet, he'd known before returning that his father would expect him to marry and set up a nursery. And Cam had promised he'd do just that.

Despite the enmity he'd forever carry for the man purported to have sired him, Cam intended to keep his promise. Because, as backward as it seemed, the one thing he'd carried with him all those years serving his country had been the burden of guilt.

He'd known his stepmother and stepsisters worried endlessly about him.

Well, not him, per se. The male son. The heir.

For the Duke of Crawford had failed to produce a spare with his second wife. She'd given birth to three girls with her first husband but failed to conceive with Crawford.

Cameron was destined to forever be the older brother to three silly stepsisters.

His conscience had berated him to do his best to avoid being killed. He'd not wished to make their circumstances precarious.

But even more compelling had been the desire to thwart the duke by living.

Cameron shook his head, dismissing the passing thought.

Hell.

And as he *had* lived, and he *had* returned, he would marry the Redfield girl.

He could only hope the girl and her sister had little memory of him and his behavior.

Upon reaching his majority, Cam had been filled with angst. He'd returned from school to discover his father remarried. The new duchess had brought with her three small daughters.

Cam had countered by drinking, carousing, swiving whatever he was offered, and then ultimately threatening to enlist himself into the British Army.

Which would have been unheard of.

An unmitigated embarrassment to the duke.

Crawford had taken the threat literally, and to avoid the disgrace, he'd negotiated a bargain with him. With the understanding that when Cam reached the age of thirty, he would return home and marry the bride of his father's choosing, the Duke of Crawford had purchased Cam an officer's commission in the British Navy,

Thirty had seemed a lifetime away.

Cam brushed a hand through his hair.

Damn his twenty-one-year-old self.

"I'm to visit the youngest daughter tomorrow?" he asked. "And she is agreeable? How old is she now?"

He certainly wouldn't force the poor girl to marry him if she was unwilling. He would make his offer, formally, dispassionately, but... pleasantly. He would not insist, however, and by God, he wouldn't beg.

"She's ten and nine. A most suitable age. We'll visit their townhouse together. For tea," his stepmother responded.

"Of course, she's agreeable. Damned fool girl she'd be if she wasn't," Crawford barked.

The girl must be a social climber then.

Hell, perhaps she'd forgotten him completely!

"Tomorrow, then? At tea." Speaking the words, he could almost hear the chains winding around his ankle.

"She's a lovely girl." The duchess patted the duke on the shoulder. "We'll allow the two of you a few moments alone, so that you can be certain you'll get on well together."

Well, then.

Damn.

"Better yet, you may renew your acquaintance this afternoon at the Snodgrass Garden Party. I wouldn't think the Redfields would miss it."

Perhaps that would make tomorrow easier. Perhaps he could charm her into forgetting his actions before he'd gone off to war. His stupid and churlish behavior.

Might make for a less awkward proposal, anyhow.

Be notified when I have a new release or sale by subscribing to my newsletter: **https://www.annabelleanders.com/newsletter-subscribe**

THE PERFECT REGENCY SERIES

The Perfect Debutante

Louella and Cameron

The Perfect Spinster

Olivia and Gabriel

The Perfect Christmas

Eliza and Henry

The Perfect Arrangement

Lillian and Christian

DEVILISH DEBUTANTES

Hell Hath No Fury

Cecily and Stephen

Hell in a Hand Basket

Sophia and Harold

Hell's Belle

Emily and Marcus

Hell of a Lady

Rhoda and Justin

Hell Hath Frozen Over (Novella)

Loretta and Thomas

To Hell and Back (Novella)

Eve and Niles

Hell's Wedding Bells (Novella)

Lila and Vincent

ABOUT THE AUTHOR

Married to the same man for over 25 years, I am a mother to three children and two Miniature Wiener dogs.

After owning a business and experiencing considerable success, my husband and I got caught in the financial crisis and lost everything in 2008; our business, our home, even our car.

At this point, I put my B.A. in Poly Sci to use and took work as a waitress and bartender (Insert irony). Unwilling to give up on a professional life, I simultaneously went back to college and obtained a degree in EnergyManagement.

And then the energy market dropped off.

And then my dog died.

I can only be grateful for this series of unfortunate events, for, with nothing to lose and completely demoralized, I sat down and began to write the romance novels which had until then, existed only my imagination. After publishing over 40 novels now, with one having been nominated for RWA's Distinguished ™RITA Award in 2019, I am happy to tell you that I have finally found my place in life.

Thank you so much for being a part of my journey!

Be notified when I have a new release or sale by subscribing to my newsletter: **https://www.annabellean ders.com/newsletter-subscribe**

www.annabelleanders.com

GET A FREE BOOK

Sign up for the news letter and download a book from Annabelle,

For **FREE!**

Sign up at **www.annabelleanders.com**

Made in the USA
Monee, IL
12 November 2025

34469955R00080